WITCHING FOR JOY

PREMONITION POINTE, BOOK 3

DEANNA CHASE

ABOUT THIS BOOK

A Paranormal Women's Fiction with a bit of class, and a lot of sass, for anyone who feels like age is just a number!

Joy Lansing is at a crossroads. Her kids have all flown the nest and just when she thought she was going to spend her golden years with her husband of thirty years, she finds herself single again and looking to rebuild a life she no longer recognizes.

Lucky for Joy she has her three besties and her coven by her side. Because she's going to need them when she lands a movie role and finds herself hexed by a jealous co-star. Finding yourself a minor film star at the age of forty-eight is more than a little overwhelming. But when it comes with bad press and a hot celebrity determined to date her, Joy is in way in over her head. She's going to need all her magic to navigate this one before her new career is over before it starts.

CHAPTER ONE

"*D*o you think a jury would acquit me if I murdered her?" Joy Lansing whispered to her makeup artist.

"I'd vote innocent," Sam Catts said as she scowled in Prissy Penderton's direction. "If she asks you about Troy Bixby one more time, I'll—"

"Joy," Prissy drawled in the sickeningly sweet voice she used when she was pretending that she and Joy were friends.

"Yes, Prissy?" Joy said, eyeing the other woman from across the makeup tent. Joy's long blond hair had already been styled into an elegant twist, and her makeup artist was working on her face for the next scene in the indie film she'd been cast in recently.

Joy's life had taken a dramatic turn after photos of her had been used in a national marketing campaign for a classic perfume line aimed at mature women. Troy Bixby, her... friend? Potential boyfriend? She wasn't sure what they were, but Troy had asked her to pose for him and the next thing she knew, her face was plastered all over the internet and in the pages of every women's magazine known to man.

The attention had been flattering and also pretty overwhelming. But when she got a call asking her to audition for a family drama that was being filmed in Premonition Pointe, that's when her lifelong dream of being an actress had come true. Joy was part of a multigenerational cast. Her character was the mother to a twenty-five-year-old and the daughter to a woman in her late sixties. All three of them come together when the granddaughter is dealing with an abusive husband through a contentious divorce and custody battle.

The script had moved Joy to tears, and she was full of pride to be a part of the project. Unfortunately, Prissy Penderton landed the lead, playing Joy's daughter. The woman had just hit stardom with a breakout role a few months before, and she'd turned out to be insufferable with her demands and entitlement. Joy stayed out of her way whenever possible. It seemed as if her luck had run out.

"I heard Troy's coming to town this weekend. You did talk to him about my cocktail party, didn't you?" Prissy asked.

Joy gritted her teeth. Prissy had been begging her to bring Troy to her cocktail party ever since the news broke that he was scheduled to be in Premonition Pointe that weekend for a gallery show. Too bad Joy had learned the news from a gossip rag and not the man himself. But the last thing she was going to do was tell the starlet that it had been more than three weeks since she'd talked to Troy. She forced a tight smile. "No, the subject hasn't come up."

"Jooooy," she whined. "I need Troy to be there or else the male-to-female ratio will be off. I'm counting on you."

"He's a busy man," Joy said with a shrug. "I'll mention it when I talk to him." *If* she talked to him. The entire world thought they were dating, thanks to a throwaway comment he'd made during an interview recently. The reporter had asked him about the gorgeous new face of Elegance, and he'd called Joy his muse. When the reporter pressed about their relationship, he'd been noncommittal, but the article had described him as having 'a sexy half-smile and a glint in his eye.'

The tabloids had run with it, calling them the hottest new "it" couple. The entire thing was making Joy question her own sanity. Because the truth was that she and Troy had spent one amazing week together heating up his sheets. During that week, he'd photographed her for the Elegance perfume campaign. Then he'd left for Europe, where he was working on his next project. He'd said he wanted to get back together when he was back in town, and while they'd sort of kept in touch, they mostly talked about his project and her new acting job. Neither of them had talked about what the future might bring when he returned home. And according to the *Premonition Perspective*, the local gossip rag, he was due back in town in just a few days.

Too bad he hadn't given her a heads-up.

"Just make sure you're both there Saturday night," Prissy insisted. "Get your hair and makeup done and dress as if you're walking the red carpet. Maybe even get some blue contacts to brighten up your eyes. Undoubtedly, the press will be there. You don't want the first photos of you after your perfume campaign to make it look like Troy's photos were heavily manipulated, do you?"

Joy scowled at the younger actress's back as Prissy retreated from the tent. Blue contacts? Her eyes were already sky blue. The younger woman was clearly enjoying pushing Joy's buttons. When she was gone, Joy looked up at her makeup artist. "She really is a bitch, right?"

"Definitely," Sam said, nodding her head. "Bitch in heat,

3

actually. I swear, if Troy does show up at her house, she's probably going to first scratch your eyes out and then pee on him."

Shaking her head, Joy let out a humorless chuckle. "She's barking up the wrong tree. He didn't even tell me he's coming to town."

Sam raised her eyebrows. "Is he ghosting on you?"

"No. We're not even dating." Joy sighed. "The media made something out of nothing. We've been in touch over the past few months, but we're not anything other than friends." Could she even call a hookup a friend? She didn't know. Dating was a foreign concept to her. Troy had been the first and only man she'd been with after her husband called it quits on their marriage. Joy hadn't been expecting anything from Troy. Why would she? It wasn't as if she was going to jump right into a relationship with a man she barely knew after a marriage that had lasted nearly three decades.

"Well then, why not just send him a text that Prissy wants him to show up at her cocktail party, and then either wash your hands of it or show up at her party looking like a million bucks and let them both eat their hearts out."

Joy glanced up at her with narrowed eyes. "And how am I going to do that?"

A slow smile claimed Sam's lips. "You let me worry about that."

"What do you have up your sleeve?" Joy asked.

She shrugged one shoulder. "Let's just say that I've got a connection to a high-profile stylist."

"Hey, *Mom*," Prissy called as she walked back into the tent carrying a mug.

Joy tried not to scowl. Her own children were right about the same age as the starlet, and she was in no way offended by the term, but it was the way Prissy said it, as if Joy's age were something to be embarrassed about, that just got under her skin.

"I brought you a coffee," Prissy said, handing Joy the mug. "Figured you could use a pick me up since it's my fault we worked so late last night."

Blinking at her, Joy wrapped her hands around the mug, stunned. Joy *was* tired. Prissy had experienced a rare off night the previous evening, and she'd caused the cast and crew to endure over fifty takes of the scene they were shooting. She'd been flat and kept forgetting her lines. The fact that she was humble enough to bring Joy coffee as a peace offering caught her off guard. It wasn't what she'd come to expect from Prissy. "Thank you. This was very kind of you."

Prissy smiled at her, did an exaggerated curtsy, and said, "That's because I *am* kind." She winked and as she left the tent again, she called over her shoulder, "Enjoy."

"That was... really weird," Sam said.

Joy had to agree. She tipped the mug to her lips and took a sip. When the rich coffee, flavored with just the right amount of creamer, hit her tongue, she nearly let out a moan of pleasure. It was exactly the way she liked it, and she decided right then and there that maybe she was being too hard on Prissy. If the woman had paid enough attention to know how Joy took her coffee, she couldn't be that bad, could she? Joy took another long sip and let out a sigh. "Damn, this is good."

"Yeah? The evil princess finally did something nice for a change?" Sam asked, applying bronzer to highlight Joy's cheekbones.

"Maybe she's turning over a new leaf," Joy said as she settled back into the chair to enjoy the rest of the coffee while Sam worked her magic.

* * *

"AND... CUT!" the director called. "That's it for today. Good job, team."

Prissy walked across the set and stopped right in front of Joy, her eyes searching Joy's face.

"It's fine," Joy said, sharply, still feeling the sting of the slap Prissy had landed in the last scene. Her cheekbone ached, but she wasn't going to give the younger actress the satisfaction of knowing she'd actually hurt her.

"I'm sure you are." Prissy narrowed her eyes and added, "You should really spend some time at that spa. Your eyes are puffy, and your complexion is a little uneven. A facial would probably do you a world of good."

Joy clenched her fists and blew out a breath, willing herself to not lash out and give the other actress a taste of her own medicine. She'd never slapped anyone in her life, but if Prissy didn't get the hell out of her face, Joy was going to unleash her frustration. How was it possible for a person to be so hot and cold? Earlier the woman had been thoughtful enough to bring her coffee, and now she was being a total bitch for reasons Joy didn't understand. "Did you need anything else?"

She shrugged one shoulder. "Just wanted to let you know you might also want to do something about that zit on your chin." Prissy smiled sweetly and then turned and trotted off to the car waiting for her.

Joy brought her hand to her chin, immediately felt the bump of the newly formed pimple, and groaned. Why had she been cursed with the most sensitive skin *and* the brattiest costar on the planet?

"Come with me," a rich, sultry voice said from behind her.

The frustration coiling in Joy's gut disappeared at the

6

sound of Carly Preston's voice. The woman was only a few years older than Joy but still had been cast to play her mother in the film. Joy wasn't unhappy about that. Carly was a renowned actress who'd won every award Hollywood offered and still managed to be the most gracious person Joy had ever met. "Where are we headed?"

"My trailer. I have something that will clear that problem right up." She smiled and slipped her arm through Joy's.

"You mean you have something that will fix Prissy's personality?" Joy asked with a gasp, grinning at the gorgeous older woman. Her hair was dyed a beautiful shade of honey blond, and she had skin so radiant that it glowed.

Carly let out a throaty laugh and her bright eyes danced with humor. "Now that really would be a miracle." She gave Joy a wry smile. "That one will have to learn the hard way that being a pill won't get her what she wants." She winked, and a moment later she invited Joy into her trailer. "Give me a second. I have a salve I get from a healer that will clear up that blemish overnight."

When Carly disappeared into the bedroom area, Joy moved to sit in one of the leather chairs but stopped when her eye caught on a cluster of framed photographs lined up on a pullout table. A tingle formed in Joy's gut and radiated to her fingers. Her feet seemed to move on their own as if she were drawn to the photos, and before she knew it, she had one of them in her hands as she stared down at a pretty young woman who had the exact same eyes as Carly Preston.

Joy thought the woman looked to be in her late twenties and that the picture hadn't been taken that long ago. She was wearing jeans and a T-shirt and was holding a smartphone in one hand, and her eyes were dancing with amusement as she blew a kiss at the camera.

It was a happy photo, but as Joy stared at it, unease clenched at her gut and her vision swam. Suddenly the picture morphed into a black-and-white scene of the woman kicking and screaming as someone dragged her from her house and into a black SUV.

Fear washed over Joy, and she let out a cry of horror as the photo slipped out of her hand, crashing to the floor.

"Joy?" Carly asked, rushing over to her, concern in her tone. "Are you okay?"

Joy was shaking as she picked up the frame and held it up for Carly to see. "Is she…" Joy swallowed hard. "Did she make it home?"

Carly stared at Joy, confused. "What do you mean, make it home?"

"She… um, I had a vision. I saw her—"

A phone rang, cutting Joy off. Carly held a hand up and smiled as she answered. "Hey Dee. What's up?" Carly's smiled vanished immediately, and worry blazed in her green eyes. "What do you mean she's gone?"

Joy paced, knowing in her gut that the phone call was somehow about the woman in the photo.

After Carly asked a few questions and assured whoever was on the other end of the line that she'd be there as fast as she could, she hung up and turned to Joy. "I think you need to tell me everything you saw in that vision." She pointed to the pretty blonde in the photo. "That's my niece Harlow, and she's just gone missing."

CHAPTER TWO

*J*oy sat in an uncomfortable plastic chair in a small conference room at the Premonition Pointe police station. There was a stale cup of coffee sitting in front of her, and the room smelled vaguely of mold and dust.

"How often do you get these visions, Mrs. Lansing?" the detective asked her.

"I don't," Joy said, knowing she was barely containing her irritation. How many times did she have to tell them this was the first time she'd ever had a vision?

"Then how did you know Ms. Preston's niece was abducted this evening?" Detective Coolidge stared at her with one eyebrow raised.

"I have no idea." Joy placed her hands down flat on the Formica table. "I've already told you that my magic is usually limited to glamor spells and telekinesis. Visions are completely new for me. I didn't even know if the vision was real until Carly got the call that Harlow was missing."

When Carly's friend Dee had gone to the house Carly had

rented to pick up her niece, Harlow, Dee had found the front door wide open. The table in the entry had been knocked over, the contents of Harlow's purse were scattered all over the front porch, and her phone had been smashed. Dee had learned that a neighbor had heard someone crying out for help, but she'd just been getting out of the shower, and by the time she made it down the stairs and to the front window, no one had been there.

"Can I go now?" Joy asked, her head pounding from the stress of the day. "I don't know anything other than what I've told you. I haven't even met Carly's niece."

The detective stood and shook her head. "No. I'm sorry, Ms. Lansing, but you're the only one who knows anything. I'm afraid you're not going anywhere this evening."

The door swung open, and another officer walked in with Carly right behind him, her eyes blazing with fire. "Detective Coolidge, you're dismissed. Please meet me in my office."

Coolidge gaped at her superior. "But Chief, the interview isn't over."

"It is now. Go."

The detective ground her teeth together, shot Joy one more glance, and said, "We'll speak again soon."

"You can try, but it's not going to change the fact that I don't know anything," Joy said, just because she was petty enough in that moment that she wanted the last word.

They all watched as the detective huffed out of the conference room.

Joy stared at the chief. "Does this mean I can go home now? Because if not, I think I'm going to have to call a lawyer."

"No one is accusing you of anything, Ms. Lansing," the chief said, his tone matter-of-fact.

"Good, then I'm free to leave." She rose from the uncomfortable chair and brushed past him.

"I'm sorry my detective was so aggressive. I assure you that she's very good at her job. Very thorough," the chief said.

Joy paused and looked over her shoulder at him. "I hope that's true for Harlow's sake. I'll be in touch if I have another vision." Though she doubted that would happen. She didn't even know why she'd had the first one. No one was more shocked than she was.

"Thank you," the chief said. "I really appreciate your help, and again, I apologize for detective Coolidge. She's just—"

"Thorough," Joy finished for the chief. "I got it." She turned to Carly. "How are you?"

"I've been better." Carly slipped her arm through Joy's. "Let's get out of here and let them do their jobs."

"I'll be in touch soon, Ms. Preston." The chief nodded to her.

Carly gave him a curt nod and then dragged Joy out of the station. Once they were outside, Carly turned to Joy. "I'm really sorry about that. I would've gotten you out of there sooner, but it took me some time to get the chief's attention."

Joy frowned at her. "What do you mean, get his attention? Wasn't he there to deal with your niece's abduction?"

"Yes, but he's coordinating all kinds of searches from canvasing to surveillance videos, and his staff was... less than helpful. If it hadn't been for a suggestion spell, we'd probably both still be in an uncomfortable plastic chair being interrogated."

"Suggestion spell?" Joy's eyes widened, and then she gave the other woman a small smile. "I didn't know you were a witch." Being a witch wasn't exactly a rarity in Premonition Pointe. The town was a magnet for those with magic. Joy was only surprised because, even though they'd been working together for a few weeks now, Carly hadn't given any indication that she was a witch.

She shrugged one shoulder. "I try not to use it on the set. That way there's no confusion that what I do is a result of my acting ability and not some spell."

Joy frowned, trying to puzzle out why magic would be a problem on the set. "How would that even work? Magic doesn't make anyone a better actor. If you used an illusion spell, the reality would show up on film."

"Some people without magic don't understand. It's just easier and cleaner to keep them separate." Carly strode across the parking lot to her rented vehicle. After Joy slid in beside her, Carly turned to her. "Do you mind coming back to the house? Maybe look at some more pictures to see if you get any more visions?"

There was a desperation in her tone that nearly ripped Joy's heart in two. Tears filled Joy's eyes as she nodded. "Of course, I will. I have to warn you that I can't promise anything. That's the first vision I've ever had."

Carly nodded solemnly. "I understand. I just… need you to try."

THE RIDE to Carly's large rental house on the south side of town was full of silence. Joy was just too drained after the day of acting and then the trauma of witnessing an abduction. If she was honest with herself, all she wanted to do was go home, drink an entire bottle of wine, and pass out so that she didn't need to think about it anymore. But she couldn't leave Carly alone, and if there was anything she could do to help, she'd do it, regardless of her own needs.

They wound their way up a steep two-lane road until finally they came to a small community of houses that overlooked a bluff. Carly steered the car to a modern house in the middle of the street and hit the garage door opener. As the door rolled up, all the windows in the house lit up, and Joy asked, "Does anyone else live here? Besides you and your niece I mean?"

Carly shook her head, and in a businesslike, emotionless tone, she said, "No. The lights are programmed to come on when the door goes up. I learned a long time ago to never walk into a dark house."

Joy studied her costar, realizing that due to her fame this might not be the first time Carly had dealt with something this serious. She wanted to ask her friend what she had meant by that statement but wasn't sure she wanted to know. Instead, she just nodded, waiting for the car to come to a stop. When it did, she slid out of the car and met Carly at the door that led into the house.

"Are you ready for this?" Joy asked her, suddenly wishing they'd asked someone to come check out the house before they went in. Someone like Hope's boyfriend, Lucas King, or maybe even just Hope, Grace, and Gigi. Her coven had proven they could handle pretty much anything. Surely they could root out an intruder if there was one. Sweat popped out on Joy's forehead, and she swallowed hard as Carly opened the unlocked door and strode in without even a hint of fear.

"Damn," Joy muttered. She really needed some of Carly's confidence. If she'd been in the lead, she'd have tiptoed in and taken forever checking every nook and cranny to be sure no one was lying in wait. Not that the tiptoeing would be needed.

It wasn't exactly a secret that someone was home, considering every light was on and the garage door was hardly silent.

"Joy?" Carly called, poking her head back into the garage. "Are you coming?"

"Of course... I was just..." Joy let her voice trail off and shook her head. "Sorry. It's been a really long day."

"Shit! Of course it has," Carly said quickly. "Did you want me to take you home? We don't have to do this—"

Joy held her hand up in a stop motion even as she hurried toward the door. "No. Time matters. Let's do this now. If I can pick anything up from your photos that can help the authorities bring her home, then it's imperative that I try as soon as possible."

"Okay," Carly said, already retreating back into the house. "That's what I was thinking, too, but I don't want you to feel pressured to do this." She averted her gaze and, in a quiet voice, added, "I'm sure it's traumatizing."

It was. Joy was sure she'd be having nightmares about the vision she'd witnessed. But she wasn't going to let that stop her. Carly's niece was missing, in the hands of only the goddess knew who, and Joy ached for her. Everything in her wished that the photos in the house would lead her right to Harlow Preston.

Joy walked through the sleek, modern beach house to stare out the window. The silver moon shone down on the churning Pacific below, and Joy walked out the glass doors to let the salty scent of the sea fill her up and recharge her magic. She'd always gotten a charge from the ocean. It was one of the reasons witches seemed to gravitate to Premonition Pointe. The night was clear with the stars illuminated above. The scene was so beautiful that it was hard to imagine a terrible crime had been committed in the house just a few hours before.

The cool wind blew in from the ocean, causing Joy to shiver. She wrapped her arms around herself and retreated back into the mostly white living room.

"The pictures are over there." Carly pointed to the mantle over a gas fireplace before gesturing to a sideboard in the dining area. "And there."

Joy made her way to the mantle and scanned the framed photos. Carly's niece was in most of them, but she narrowed in on a joyful shot of the vibrant young woman. She was on the beach, her head thrown back as she laughed. Joy trailed her fingers over the glass as if tracing the picture. She cleared her mind and thought only of the woman reflected back at her and waited.

And waited.

And waited some more.

Nothing. No vision. There wasn't even a tingle of magic.

Joy sighed and put the picture back on the mantle. Maybe her magic was the issue. Hadn't she felt that tingle of magic last time right before the vision? She thought so, but so much had happened since then that she wasn't sure.

She reached for another photo. In this one Harlow was standing on the beach, her head bowed as the waves crashed around her feet. Joy thought of the water and conjured enough magic that her skin started to tingle. But even as her magic flared to life, it didn't bring any visions. Instead, it just slipped away.

"Any luck?" Carly asked from behind her.

Joy replaced the second photo and shook her head as she turned to face her costar. "I'm afraid not. I don't even know if it's something I can will myself to do. The last one came out of nowhere."

Carly frowned, looking disappointed, but she nodded. "I was afraid of that. Do you mind trying a few more times?"

"Not at all." Joy desperately wanted to help her find Harlow. The younger woman's abduction weighed on her, and she felt like she was letting both Carly and her niece down by not being able to do more. She spent the next half hour staring at every picture in Carly's beach house before she finally flopped down on the white couch and let out a frustrated groan. "I think it's time I admit defeat."

Carly placed a silver tea service on the coffee table and took a seat in the armchair across from her. After she poured water into the two cups, she handed one of them to Joy. "I understand. Thank you for trying."

There was so much disappointment in Carly's tone, it made Joy hesitant to give up on trying to find Harlow. But the visions just weren't coming. "What do you think about me calling my coven? If we were all together, we might be able to make something happen."

"Your coven? Do you think they would come?" There was so much hope in Carly's voice that Joy almost felt guilty for suggesting it. There wasn't any reason to believe her coven sisters could do anything to find Harlow, but she just couldn't give up yet.

"I'm sure they will if they're available—" Joy started, but then she stopped abruptly when her phone started to play "Sweet Child O' Mine" by Guns and Roses, indicating it was one of her kids. "Give me just a sec." She fished her phone out of her pocket, accepted the call, and said, "Hey, Kyle. What's up?"

There was silence on the other end.

"Kyle?" she said again, frowning. "You there?"

"Yeah. I'm here." His voice was shaky as he added, "I'm okay, but I need you to come. I'm in the hospital."

Joy's chest tightened, and her head started to spin until she realized that she'd stopped breathing and sucked in a shaky breath. "What happened?"

"Car accident."

"I'll be right there." She ended the call and turned to Carly. "I have to go. My son..." She trailed off, realizing she had no idea what Kyle's injuries were. "He's been in an accident. I'm sorry about—" She waved a hand, indicating the photos.

Carly shook her head and grabbed her keys and then Joy's hand as she tugged her toward the garage. "Don't worry about that. Come on. I'll take you to him."

CHAPTER THREE

*J*oy rushed into the emergency room of Pointe Memorial hospital, singularly focused on finding her youngest child. She quickly scanned the waiting room and then hurried to the admissions window. Just as she reached the counter, she did a double take when she recognized Jackson, one of Kyle's best friends. His normally tamed dark curly hair was sticking up in all directions as if he'd just woken up and rushed to the hospital. It wasn't that late, was it? She'd just stopped behind him when she heard the receptionist ask if Jackson was family.

Joy was about to say yes but was shocked into silence when Jackson spoke.

"I'm his boyfriend." Jackson sniffed as if he'd been crying. "Please. I need to make sure he's all right."

"Normally we only allow family in," the nurse said.

"But—" Jackson started.

"Excuse me," Joy said softly.

Jackson stiffened, and when he turned around, there was a look of horror on his beautiful face. "Mrs. Lansing, I—"

"It's okay, Jackson." Her mom instincts kicked in, and she gave him a reassuring smile before turning to the receptionist. "I'm Kyle's mother. Can we see him now?"

"Just a moment." The receptionist left the desk area and retreated behind a door that Joy assumed led to the restricted part of the hospital.

"Mrs. Lansing, I'm so sorry." Jackson's gaze darted around the waiting room, looking at anything other than Joy. "I thought if I told them I was his boyfriend that they might let me back to see him. I know it's supposed to be family only, but the tow truck guy told me the ambulance took him and I—"

"Ambulance?" Joy cried. "Just how bad is it? What happened?"

Jackson swallowed and, in a small voice, said, "I don't know for sure. We were on the phone having a… disagreement. Kyle was yelling at me and then suddenly he cried out, and all I heard was screeching and..." He shook his head. "He was headed home from his dad's, so I knew the route and went to find him. By the time I found his car, it was being towed and he'd already been brought to the hospital. It looked like he sideswiped a tree."

Joy's entire body went cold at the thought that her son had hit a tree. He could've killed himself. *But he didn't*, she told herself. He'd called her. He'd been coherent. Whatever his injuries, they couldn't be life threatening, could they? "Do you know his injuries?"

He shook his head as his eyes filled with unshed tears. "I'm so sorry, Mrs. Lansing. We shouldn't have been on the phone while he was driving. It's my fault."

Joy reached over and wrapped her arm around his shoulders, pulling him into her. "First, you know you're supposed to call me Joy. Second, you are not responsible for Kyle's actions. Was he at least handsfree?"

He leaned into her, his body shaking. "Yeah. He was using Bluetooth."

She let out the breath she'd been holding and ran her hand up and down his arm, comforting him. Honestly, the fact that she had someone to take care of was easing some of her own anxiety. "That's good. It's not your fault," she insisted again.

Jackson pulled away and opened his mouth to say something more but was cut off when the receptionist returned. "You may go back now. Exam room six on the left."

Joy grabbed Jackson's hand and tugged him through the doors and down the corridor. When Joy entered her son's room, she suppressed a gasp of horror when she saw her handsome golden boy. There was a cut on his head and bruises on the left side of his face. His left pant leg had been ripped open and his leg was wrapped with an elastic bandage. Joy rushed to his side and took his right hand in both of hers. "Hey, baby," she said, giving him a small smile but unable to hide the tremble in her voice. She couldn't help it. Her youngest was hurt.

Kyle let out a soft groan. "I'm okay, Mom. Don't freak out."

"I'm not freaking out," she insisted. "I am concerned about you though. How are you really?" She glanced at his leg. "That doesn't look good."

He shook his head. "It's broken. They're going to set it soon and then discharge me."

"Broken?" Jackson gasped out.

Kyle's green eyes shifted to Jackson. They stared at each other for a moment, and Joy frowned when she saw something painful and raw pass between them.

"I'm sorry," Jackson said softly. "It's my fault."

Kyle let out another groan and ran a hand through his thick honey-colored hair. "No, it isn't, Jay. And I'm sorry, too." He squeezed his eyes shut and winced as he covered his left eye with his hand. "I think my face hit the window."

"Did they give you painkillers?" Jackson asked, moving to the other side of the bed. He reached out as if he were going to grab Kyle's free hand but then stopped and clutched the bed railing instead.

Joy watched the two young men, wondering just what exactly was going on between them. They'd been friends for years, but had it turned into something more? There was definitely something between them. Had Jackson's claim that he was Kyle's boyfriend been the truth? If so, why had he told her he'd just said that to get in to see him? She'd known Jackson was gay for years and had always accepted him, no questions asked. Was he protecting Kyle? Her son had dated plenty of girls, and she'd never suspected he might be interested in men.

"Kyle?" Joy asked.

He pulled his gaze from Jackson and stared at her. "Yeah?"

"Did they give you painkillers?" she asked, deciding that whatever was happening between Kyle and Jackson could wait. She needed to know the extent of her son's injuries.

"Yeah. I think they must be kicking in because I'm getting a little spacey." He gave her a half smile and winced again, this time touching the left side of this lips. "Ouch."

"Okay. Broken leg, bruising, anything else I need to know?"

He shook his head slightly. "No. I don't think so."

She nodded. "Did you call your dad?" Joy realized she should've called Paul the minute she'd gotten off the phone with Kyle, but she'd been so panicked and rattled after the day's events that she hadn't even thought of him.

"No!" he said sharply. "I don't want him here."

Joy's eyes widened at the outburst. Even though she and Paul were in the middle of a divorce, they'd been careful to keep their kids out of it. Not that the separation was messy. If anything, it was the most amicable divorce Joy had ever heard of. Paul had moved out. They'd worked out an agreement with an arbitrator, and that was it. All that was left was waiting on the state to make it official. Their three kids were grown, so there wasn't any custody or alimony to work out. They done well over the years, so even though the assets were split fifty-fifty, both of them had ended up in a good place financially. "What happened, Kyle? Did you and your father have a falling out?"

"Falling out," Kyle scoffed. "You could call it that."

Joy sank down into the plastic chair next to his bed. "What did you argue about?"

Kyle glanced over at Jackson and then turned back to Joy. But before he could say anything else, the door swung open and the doctor walked in.

"Are you ready to get that leg set, Kyle?" the doctor asked with a kind smile.

Relief washed over his pained face, and he nodded.

"You must be Kyle's mom," the doctor said, holding her hand out to Joy. "He's a little beat up, but the good news is that he doesn't need surgery. We can set the leg without that."

"How long will I be in the cast?" Kyle asked.

"First we'll fit you with an air cast until the swelling goes down. Then you'll be in the regular one for about six weeks if everything goes well. After that, we'll move to a boot while you continue to heal. But while you're in the cast, you'll need to stay off it completely."

"He lives in a second-story apartment," Joy said. "No elevator."

"That's not ideal. Going up and down those stairs will be precarious on crutches. And if he reinjures it, it could mean surgery."

Kyle groaned.

Joy patted her son's arm. "Looks like I'll have a roommate for a while." She turned to the doctor. "He'll come home with me."

"Glad to hear it." She made a note in her chart. "We're going to take Kyle to get that cast on, and as soon as we're done, you can take him home."

Two orderlies arrived, and a few minutes later, they were rolling Kyle out of the room.

When Joy and Jackson were alone, Joy studied the normally outspoken young man whose personality was usually larger than life. His face was white, and he looked shaken. "He's going to be okay. You know that, right?"

Jackson nodded. "Yeah. He scared me there for a minute though. I heard the crash on the phone and..." He shook his head. "I'm not sure I'm ever going to forget that."

A shudder ran through Joy as she imagined her son's car hitting that tree. It felt like a punch in the gut, and her chest ached with the realization that the outcome could've been so much worse. She shook her head. The last thing she needed to do was worry about what hadn't happened. She cleared her throat and changed the subject. "So, you and Kyle? Is everything okay there?"

He glanced away. "I'm sorry, I can't talk about this, Mrs. Lansing."

"Call me Joy," she insisted again.

"Right. Joy." He took a seat across the room from her and stared at his feet.

Joy sighed. And then because she had to make sure he knew where she stood, she said, "I don't want to make any assumptions here, and I'm not asking you to tell me anything, but if there is something more than friendship between you and my son, I'm completely okay with it."

He blinked, and his mouth worked as if he were trying to figure out what to say.

Joy held her hand up. "Really, don't say anything. I'm certain if there is something for me to know, it's a conversation I should be having with Kyle whenever he's ready for it. I just wanted to make myself clear, okay?"

Jackson nodded and then smiled. "Okay."

Joy stood and made her way across the room. The boy she'd known since he was five years old looked up at her. She smiled down at him and opened her arms wide. "I think it's time for a hug, don't you?"

He let out a chuckle and got to his feet, embracing her in a bear hug. "I love you, Mrs. L."

It was what his mom had told him to call her when he was little, so she didn't correct him again. Instead, she held him tightly and said, "Thank you for being here for Kyle. I love you, too."

CHAPTER FOUR

The phone rang, startling Joy out of a deep sleep. She sat straight up in bed and glanced around, looking for her phone through blurry eyes. It had been late when she and Kyle got home the night before, and by the time she got him settled back in his old room, it had been well past three in the morning. Then it had taken a couple hours for her to finally get to sleep.

She wiped the sleep from her eyes and squinted at her clock. It was just past eight. Three hours wasn't nearly enough. She grabbed her phone, glanced at the screen, and then answered. "Grace? What's wrong?"

"Nothing's wrong here," her best friend said impatiently over the line. "I'm calling to find out why I had to hear from Lex that Kyle was in a car accident. Is he okay? What happened?"

Joy yawned, but then her lips curled into a tiny smile. It was good to have friends who cared so much. She just hadn't thought the rumor mill would've been spinning quite that early. But then she should've known it wouldn't take long for

Grace to learn about the accident. Her niece, Lex, was good friends with both Jackson and Kyle. Jackson had probably called her the night before. It wouldn't have taken long for Lex to call Grace. "He's okay. Or at least he was last night when I put him to bed."

"He's there at the house?" Grace asked.

Joy nodded even though Grace couldn't see her as she climbed out of bed and dug around in her dresser for her favorite yoga pants. "Yep. He'll be here for a while. He has a fractured tibia and is in a cast. He's not supposed to put any weight on it, and those stairs at his apartment just aren't going to cut it until he gets some of his mobility back."

"I'm coming over. I'll make you guys breakfast," Grace insisted.

"Grace, you don't have to do that. I'll—"

"How much sleep did you get last night?" Grace asked.

Joy heard a door slam on the other end of the line as she said, "Not enough."

"That's what I thought. Don't try to talk me out of it. I'm already on my way. I'll be there in fifteen."

The call ended, and Joy felt her heart swell a little. What had she done to deserve such a good friend? She glanced at her phone, checking for a message from the production assistant who texted her every day with any changes to the filming schedule. Sure enough, they'd rearranged filming to give Carly a few days off, and that meant Joy didn't need to be there until the afternoon. She let out a relieved sigh that she wouldn't be working a long day.

After brushing her teeth and running a brush through her hair, Joy made her way into her large kitchen and went straight for the coffee pot. There was no way she was getting through the day without copious amounts of caffeine. Once she had the pot going, she went to Kyle's room and knocked softly. When there was no response, she cracked the door open and peeked inside. When she noted that Kyle was missing from the bed, she opened the door wider and called, "Kyle?"

There was no answer. Of course there wasn't. His bedroom didn't have an en suite bathroom. Where exactly did Joy expect him to be? Hiding in the closet?

She walked through the four-bedroom house where she'd spent the last thirty years raising her family, checking each room for her youngest child. Now that her marriage was over and each of her children had moved out, the place was far too big for just her, but she hadn't considered moving. The beach was just a few blocks away, and she'd turned her backyard into a haven with a lush garden, outdoor firepit, and a porch swing where she'd spent many hours reading.

And the backyard was exactly where she found her son.

Her lanky, blond-haired kid was sitting wrapped in a quilt on her swing, holding a paper coffee cup from the Pointe of View Café. He was slumped down with his left leg propped up on one of the other deck chairs. "Hey," she said softly, taking a seat on the other side of him.

He'd quickly moved the excess blanket covering the bench seat, and when she was settled, he offered it to her.

"Thanks, sonny boy." Joy draped the blanket over her thighs and smiled at him, trying not to wince at the purple bruises all up and down his face. She nodded at the cup. "Did the coffee fairy drop that off for you?"

He snorted. "You could say that. Jackson gave it to Lex to bring by when she stopped in this morning."

"Lex has already been here?" she asked.

He nodded. "She had an interview for the assistant manager

position at Point of View this morning. She thinks it went well."

"Really? That's good." Lex was a recent college graduate in hospitality management. But finding a job in her field had been challenging, and she'd spent the last six months working at her girlfriend's family deli.

"I hope she gets it. She'd be great." He took another sip of his coffee as he stared straight ahead. But she was certain he wasn't seeing her late-blooming sunflowers. He was lost in his own thoughts.

"How's your leg today? Were you able to get much sleep?" she asked, gently placing her hand on his right knee.

Kyle shook his head. "Not really. I drifted in and out, but even with the pain medication, the dull ache and awkwardness of the cast kept me from really sleeping."

"I'm sorry, honey. I know everything is awful right now. But it will get better." She hated that her reassurances sounded so dismissive. "I'm sure it sucks to be back at home with your mom taking care of you."

He lifted his gaze to hers and in a quiet voice said, "I don't mind. It's kind of nice to be home, actually."

She blinked at him and then chuckled. "Really? I'm sure in a few days you'll be dying to get out of here."

He just shrugged and went back to staring at her garden.

Joy swallowed a sigh because she could tell there was something more than just his injuries bothering him. She hadn't seen that look on his face since his girlfriend broke up with him the day before his seventeenth birthday. He was heartbroken, but she had no idea over who. "Kyle?"

"Yeah?" He lifted his gaze to hers.

"Is there something you need to talk about?" If he was

heartbroken, surely it wasn't over Jackson since he'd sent Kyle coffee that morning.

He closed his eyes and slumped further into the swing.

Joy waited, knowing her son would only talk when he was ready. She could often get her two other kids to open up just by prodding them. But Kyle? No. He was the sensitive one who internalized everything and then eventually came to her on his own terms.

"Did you call Hunter and Britt?" he asked.

"Not yet." She eyed his coffee cup and wished desperately that she'd waited for her pot to be done before heading outside. Her head was fuzzy, and she could really use a shot of caffeine.

He apparently noticed her longing and held the cup out to her.

Joy reached for it gratefully and took a long sip of the over-sugared latte. But that hint of caffeine was exactly what she needed. "It was late when we got home. I did call your father, though."

Kyle's body tensed, and his eyes flashed with anger as he looked at her accusingly. "I told you I didn't want to call him."

"Actually," she said mildly, "you told me you didn't want to see him. Which was a request we are both honoring."

"I'm sure it's a real hardship for dad," Kyle said sarcastically. "It's not like he wanted to be a part of this family anyway."

Mild shock jolted through Joy at his outburst. But she really shouldn't have been surprised. The separation had come as a shock to all of them. It was normal for her kids to have resentment. Still, she wanted them to have a relationship with their father, so she found herself defending him. "Just because we're getting a divorce, it doesn't mean your dad is leaving the family, Kyle. You know that. He's still around. We're just not living together anymore."

Kyle gave her an incredulous look. "Seriously, Mom? He left you. He didn't even give you a real reason. Hell, he didn't give *us* a real reason. He just said you two grew apart and it wasn't good to stay in a marriage where two people aren't connected anymore. What the hell kind of bullshit is that? We all know you didn't ask him to leave. So now because he doesn't want to work on whatever it is, he just left. And we're expected to do every holiday twice. Once with you and once with him. We won't ever have family dinners with us all together, and what about other life events? Will he even show up? You know we've barely seen him since he moved out. It's just totally fucked up!"

Joy winced at the sound of her youngest swearing but didn't say anything about his language. He was right. About all of it. "You don't have to do every holiday twice. We can switch off and—"

"Mom!" He pushed himself up to sit straighter and glared at her. But when he spoke again, his voice was softer. "Don't think for a minute we're not coming home for Christmas or Thanksgiving. This is our home. And you're the one who always makes the holidays special anyway."

Tears filled her eyes, and she didn't bother to blink them away. She'd been doing okay with the divorce. Paul had been so emotionally distant the last few years that she'd almost been relieved when he said he was leaving. But when it came to her family, she was heartbroken that Paul had given up on them. And the vision she'd had of their future, growing old together, being grandparents, filling their home with love, had been forever altered. Paul had been a good father. They'd been in love once. It killed her that she didn't know what happened.

And it killed her that her son and likely her other two children were in pain, too. Just because they were older, it didn't mean they didn't care that their parents' marriage had ended.

"Please don't cry," Kyle said, looking anxious. "I'm sorry. I didn't mean to upset you."

"You didn't. I—I'm happy that you love being here for the holidays. That's all," she said, wiping her tears away.

"Really?" Kyle raised one skeptical eyebrow.

She let out a soft chuckle, admitting defeat. "Okay, maybe I am a little upset. I am touched that you love spending the holidays here, but I'm also sad that the future we'd all hoped for looks different now. I'm sure your father is, too. But as upset as you are that things are different now, that doesn't change the fact that he loves you. He didn't divorce you and Hunter and Britt, you know."

"Not yet," Kyle said, his expression turning dark again.

"Are you ready to talk about what happened with your father last night?" Joy asked.

Kyle looked down at Joy's hand covering his. "We just got into an argument; that's all."

"About what? The divorce?" she asked.

"Yes. No." He shrugged. "It was everything. He wanted to know when I was going to apply to law school, and I told him I didn't know if that's what I wanted to do anymore. Then he got pissed and accused me of thinking with something other than my head."

Joy sat back in the swing, trying to process what her son had just told her. He'd recently graduated with a degree in English. She knew he was considering law school, but not that he'd decided against it. "What did your father mean when he said you were thinking with something other than your head? Are you dating someone here in Premonition Pointe?"

His face flushed, and he glanced away. When he turned back to her, he said, "I've been dating, but that's not the reason I don't want to go away. I just decided law isn't for me." He paused and then added, "I got an interview at *Premonition Pointe News*. It's supposed to be Monday morning."

"You did?" Joy exclaimed. "That's wonderful. You'd be great at that."

Relief flooded his face, and he gave her a small smile. "I thought that's what you'd say, but Dad told me being a journalist for a small hometown paper is a waste of time with no room for career growth. He basically told me I'd be throwing my education away by working there."

"He said what?" A spark of anger shot down her spine. And before he could say anything, she plowed on with her outrage. "How dare he? Money isn't everything. And there's a career in writing. You could freelance or work on a book or anything you want to do. Plus, you're still waiting tables and working on the weekends with the adventure company, right?"

He nodded, his smile faltering slightly. "I was. But it's going to be hard to lead ATV rides or wait tables with a broken leg."

Joy winced. "Right." Then she waved a hand. "I'm sure there will be a spot for you at both places once your leg heals. In the meantime, since you're on a month-to-month rental at your apartment, you could let it go while you're recovering here. That will save you some money."

"I wasn't planning on moving out of my apartment." He swallowed, and she could see that moving home wasn't at all what he wanted to do. "I have some savings. It's only six weeks that I'll be here, right?"

"That's what the doctor said. It's your savings. If that's what you want to do, then okay. If you want to save it, I have four bedrooms, free rent, and free homecooked meals."

He ran a hand through his hair and then narrowed his eyes at her. "Is this you angling to get me to move back in with you permanently?"

Joy threw her head back and laughed. "No, sonny boy. I admit that I like having you around, but I'm not trying to manipulate you into doing something you don't want to do. I'm trying to help you. If money is an issue, you know you can always land here."

"That should be great for dating," he muttered.

Once again, she wondered if there was something more than friendship between him and Jackson. Should she say something about it? Make it clear she was perfectly fine with it? But why would he think otherwise? Lex had a girlfriend, and that had never been an issue, and Kyle knew that she was aware Jackson was gay and had never treated him any differently. She quickly decided it was better to just leave it alone. She'd already told Jackson where she stood. Surely, if they were in a relationship, he'd tell Kyle what she'd said. There was no need to put pressure on her son to tell her something he might not be ready to talk about. Joy shifted gears and thought of her own dating life and wondered for the hundredth time when she'd hear from Troy.

"Speaking of dating," Kyle said as if he'd read her mind. "What's going on with you and the photographer?"

It was Joy's turn to shrug. "Nothing."

"That's not what the tabloids say," he said with a glint of humor in his eyes.

She chuckled. "Can't believe everything you read." Then she sobered. "Honestly, we're just friends. There's not anything to talk about there."

"We'll see."

She was about to ask him what that meant, but the back

door swung open and Hope and Grace poured out of her house and rushed over to them, each of them fussing over Kyle, wanting to make sure he was all right.

It didn't take long before he was yawning and insisting he needed to lie down for a while.

Joy rose from the swing and handed him his crutches. "Can I get you anything?"

"Water? Maybe some toast so I can take my pain meds?"

"I'm on it," Hope said, turning and rushing back into the house, her dark curls flying behind her.

Grace held the door open for Kyle, and Joy waited patiently while her youngest child hobbled back into the house.

CHAPTER FIVE

"You look beat," Hope said, eyeing Joy from the other side of the kitchen table. She'd swept her dark curls up into a messy bun. Her whiskey-colored eyes were scrutinizing Joy's face. "Did you get any sleep last night?"

Joy held her hand up, covering her mouth as she yawned so hard her eyes watered. "A little. It was a very long day."

Grace Valentine placed a plate of pumpkin-spice pancakes in front of Joy.

Joy glanced up at her friend and marveled that she was so well put together. She was wearing a chic shimmering-blue pant suit, and her wavy auburn hair was styled to perfection. "Thank you. You look fantastic. Got a big day?"

Grace grinned. "I have a new high-end client, and I'm showing him the Emsworth estate."

The Emsworth estate was a large private home ten miles south of town with its own private beach. If Grace sold that property, the commission would be spectacular. "No wonder you dressed in your fancy duds. Did you bring your lucky heels? They'd go perfectly with that suit."

Grace smiled at her friend. "They're in the car."

"Perfect. It sounds like you're on track to earn that Realtor of the Year title." Joy winked at her and dug into her pancakes. She took a bite and let out a moan of pleasure.

The conversation ceased as they each tucked into their breakfasts. When Joy finally put her fork down and leaned back in her chair, resting her hands on her full stomach, Grace asked, "Are you going to tell us what happened yesterday?"

Joy flicked her gaze over her two friends and said, "You heard about Harlow Preston." Then she narrowed her eyes at Hope. "Or did you read my mind?"

Hope held both hands up in a stop motion. "Nope. No listening in like Angela does," she said, referring to her mother, who was unable to stop reading minds. She had no control over it, unlike Hope, who was learning she could close her senses and keep the thoughts of others out sometimes. "I'd tell you if I did. But it doesn't happen that often. Mostly it's just when there are a lot of people around and I get overloaded or if my emotions are all over the place. It was in the *Premonition Perspective* this morning," Hope said with a scowl. "It said you were held at the police station and questioned for hours. I swear, that rag is getting worse and worse."

Joy let out a gasp. "It was in a gossip column?"

Hope nodded. "I only know because Lucas's mom likes to read the stories out loud every morning. Imagine my surprise when she rattled off that Joy Lansing was seen being escorted into the police station after Carly Preston's niece had gone missing." Hope had recently moved into her dream home with her fiancé and his mother. It was quite a departure for Hope, who'd always been the most independent of the trio. But her life with Lucas clearly agreed with her, and Joy had never seen her friend so happy and content.

Joy buried her face in her hands and let out a groan. "Oh shit. What if the national gossip rags pick that up? Gods. They could've at least gotten the details as to why I was there instead of making it sound like I'm a suspect."

"Look at it this way," Grace said with a kind smile. "Maybe it'll give you street cred and Prissy will finally leave you alone."

Joy couldn't help it. She let out a snort of laughter and said, "One can only hope." Then she sobered, because there was nothing funny about Harlow's disappearance. She took a long sip of coffee and then carefully set the mug back on the table as she tried to breathe through the fresh anxiety.

"So, why were you there?" Hope asked, sipping from her own mug.

"Have either of you ever had a vision?" Joy asked.

"What do you mean by a vision? I heard a message at the bluff that one night right before I got the job with Landers Realty," Grace said.

"I heard a message there, too, right before my birthday," Hope added.

The messages her two friends had heard were a pretty normal occurrence for the town. There was a reason it was called Premonition Pointe. The sea was a siren call for witches who were facing change, and often, if a witch let herself communicate with nature, she'd hear a message or premonition of what was to come. "This wasn't anything like that. I was just looking at a picture of Carly's niece, and the next thing I knew I was pulled into a vision of her and watched helplessly as she was abducted from the house they're sharing. It felt like it was happening in real time, and there was absolutely nothing I could do but watch."

"Holy gods," Grace whispered, pressing her hand to her throat. "That must've been terrifying."

Joy nodded. It most definitely had been terrifying, and it was the reason she hadn't gotten much sleep the night before after making sure Kyle was okay. Every time she closed her eyes, she saw Harlow being dragged off through the night. "I actually was getting ready to call you two and Gigi last night to see if we could combine our magic for some sort of information or finding spell, but then I got the call that Kyle was in the hospital and..." She shrugged. "Obviously he was my priority."

Grace glanced down the hallway toward the bedrooms. "How is he really doing?"

Before they'd sat down for breakfast, Kyle had gone back to bed and taken another pain pill. The last time Joy had checked on him, he'd finally been asleep. "Not great. He had an argument with Paul yesterday about his career goals. Kyle decided he doesn't want to go to law school and wants to try to be a writer. He has an interview with the paper on Monday."

"He does? That's great!" Hope said, smiling wide. "I have some contacts there. I'll see if I can put in a good word for him." Hope was an event planner and sent out press releases for town events regularly. It wasn't a surprise she had connections there.

"Thanks, Hope," Joy said, squeezing her friend's hand. "It's too bad his father couldn't have lent that kind of support."

Grace groaned. "Oh, no. What did Paul say?"

Joy smirked. Of course her friend already new Paul had been a jackass. Why was it they'd always seen what she couldn't about her soon-to-be ex? "He was pissed Kyle decided not to pursue his law degree and told him being a writer would doom him to a life of poverty."

"Elitist snob," Hope said, shaking her head.

"What's wrong with being a writer?" Grace asked. "I know the paper probably doesn't pay well, but he can freelance and work for all kinds of publications without ever leaving Premonition Pointe. Or there's always books and ghostwriting. Or technical writing even."

Joy smiled at her friends. "You're right. I said something similar." She glanced at Hope. "Though I kept the elitist snob part to myself. No need to stoke the tension further."

Hope snorted. "I guess, but it's not like Kyle's dumb. He knows his father is being a dick."

"Obviously. He was pretty upset when he left his house." Joy poked her fork at the leftover pancakes on her plate. "I don't know what happened to Paul. He didn't used to be that bad. I know he just wants to make sure the kids are set up to succeed, but this is the first time he hasn't been fully supportive of something one of them wanted to do."

"Have you talked to him yet?" Grace asked, drumming her fingers on the table.

"Just long enough to tell him about the accident. We didn't talk about anything else," Joy answered.

"I think you need to tell him what his attitude is going to do to his relationship with Kyle," Grace said. "Not for him. For Kyle."

Joy groaned. "You're right, but it really sucks that I still need to be the go-between."

Grace reached over and grabbed Joy's hand and squeezed as Hope placed hers over both of their hands in support.

"Thank you both for being here today and taking care of me," Joy said as tears stung the backs of her eyes. "It's been a rough twenty-four hours."

"Always," Grace said, checking her watch. She stood. "I have to get going, but do you want to still get together with Gigi? I'm more than willing to get the coven together to see if we can work out a spell to help track down Harlow. In fact, I can't think of a better reason to use our powers."

"Yes. Can you call Gigi on your way to your appointment and see if she's free?" Joy asked her.

"I'm on it." She bent down and kissed Joy on the cheek and gave Hope a quick hug from behind. "You two stay out of trouble. I'm going to go make sure my client is dazzled enough to write an offer." She winked and strode out of the house.

"She's really come into her own," Joy said, turning her attention to Hope. "I've never seen her look and act so confident."

"It appears divorce was good for her," Hope agreed. "You know, I see the same changes in you." She grinned at Joy. "Or at least I usually do. Today you look a little like a troll who hasn't slept in two years."

Joy rolled her eyes. "Oh, shut up. Let's see how you look after spending half the night in the emergency room."

Hope chuckled and started clearing the table. Joy rose and swayed on her feet from the lack of sleep.

"Oh, no you don't," Hope said, steadying Joy. "You go lay back down and get a nap before you need to be on set, and I'll take care of this."

Joy glanced at her clock. She still had a few hours before she needed to be on set, and the pillow was calling her name. "Are you sure?" Joy asked her.

"Positive. You get a catnap, and I'll take care of everything, including keeping an eye on Kyle in case he wakes up and needs anything."

"Thanks." Joy made a stop at the refrigerator for a bottle of water and then grabbed the newspaper one of them had brought in. She glanced at the front page, spotted a black and white photo of Harlow, and let out a gasp as images of the young woman filled her mind.

Harlow was lying on a large king-size bed that was covered in a princess pink comforter and piles of red and pink pillows. The walls were painted the same overwhelming pink color, and in the corner, an oversized white chair faced the window. Joy focused on the view, trying her best to commit the impeccable rose garden to memory.

"No!" Harlow cried out as she thrashed on the bed. It was then that Joy noticed both her hands and feet were tied together.

Fear crawled down Joy's spine, but she knew instinctively that it wasn't her own fear. It was Harlow's.

"Joy?" Hope's voice sounded far away.

"Huh?" Joy said, hearing the gravel in her voice.

"Come on. Let's get you up and to your room."

Joy forced her eyes open and stared up at Hope, who was hovering over her.

"There you are," her friend said with a reassuring smile.

Joy glanced around and realized she was splayed out on her floor. "Oh, gods. Did I pass out?"

"I think so. You're probably just overly tired. If you get some sleep—"

"Hope, I had another vision of Harlow."

"What? While you were passed out?" She frowned, and then her expression cleared for a moment before turning to one of pure rage. "She's locked in a room with her hands and feet bound?"

Joy nodded, realizing that her friend had just read her mind. She wasn't surprised. Joy's emotions were running higher than usual, and Hope's probably were too since she'd just witnessed her friend pass out. Joy pushed herself up and took Hope's hand as she got to her feet. "She's in some posh room. Whoever has her, has money."

"Do you think it's someone Carly knows?" Hope asked.

Joy shrugged. "Maybe? I don't know. But I need to talk to her." Joy tugged her phone out of her pocket and called her costar. It went straight to voicemail. She tried a couple more times with no luck. "I think she turned her phone off. I need to go over there. This can't wait."

Hope chewed on her bottom lip, and Joy was positive her friend was going to try to stop her, but then Hope nodded. "I'll drive you. But not before we get some sugar in you."

"Sugar? Why? I just ate." Joy was already moving down the hall to check on Kyle before they left.

"Because you just passed out, and it seems like a good idea."

Joy rolled her eyes, already feeling better. She was sure the combination of the vision and her lack of sleep was what had done her in. "Fine. There's a bag of chocolate in the pantry behind the flour cannister." She heard Hope rummaging around in the kitchen as she knocked softly on Kyle's door. When he didn't respond, she cracked the door open and found him passed out on his back, his face slack with sleep. She let out a sigh of relief and sent a text for him to find in case he woke while they were gone.

CHAPTER SIX

"It's a freakin' circus out here," Hope said as she pulled her SUV to a stop a few blocks from Carly's rented home.

Joy peered out of the window at the dozens of paparazzi lined up outside her costar's home and groaned. There were a lot of things she loved about the acting business, but the lack of privacy wasn't one of them. It honestly made her second guess her decision to be a part of the business. Not that the photographers were lined up outside of her home, but she'd been in the press enough to get an inkling of how invasive it could be. She could only imagine what Carly was going through at the moment. She pushed her door open. "Come on. There's no use trying to wait them out. It's not going to get any better."

Hope followed without comment. It didn't take long before cameras were shoved in their faces. They all started shouting at her at once.

"Joy, why did the police hold you at the station last night?"

"Ms. Lansing, do you have a comment about Harlow's disappearance?"

"Can you tell us where the investigation stands?"

"There are reports that Carly Preston is having a nervous breakdown. Can you confirm that allegation?"

Joy grimaced and did her best to ignore all of them. When they got to the sidewalk leading to the front door, two large men wearing all black, one bald and the other with dark curls, stepped in to block their path.

"Ms. Preston isn't expecting any visitors," the bald one said.

"Can you please tell her that Joy is here and that I have information she's going to want to hear," Joy said.

"I'm sorry. No visitors," Baldy said again.

Joy gritted her teeth. "Look. I'm sure Carly doesn't want to see anyone. I tried to call her, but she's either turned her phone off or thrown it in the ocean, because it's going straight to voicemail. I'd have left a message, but her box is full. I'm a friend and fellow actor who's in the same movie she's in. I'm the one who was with her last night when she found out her niece had been abducted. I now have more information that she needs. I'm willing to bet my entire paycheck for the movie we're making that if you turn me away, she's going to be livid when she finds out later. Trust me. You want to at least let her know I'm here."

The two guards stared at each other for a moment, until Curls shrugged and said, "I'll go speak with her."

"I think that's a great idea. Joy Lansing."

He didn't acknowledge that she'd spoken; he just turned on his heel and strode up to the front door.

Baldy eyed Joy and then Hope. His gaze lingered on Hope's lush figure, and his lips curved into a half-smile. "You're a sexy one, aren't you?"

Hope rolled her eyes. "What is this, a pick-up bar?"

He shrugged. "I don't get out to bars much these days. And I've found it pays to just take the opportunities when they present themselves." He winked at her and held out a business card. "Give me a call if you're ready for me to rock your world."

Joy blinked at the man, totally taken aback by his hubris.

Hope just shook her head. "Nice try, but I'm engaged." She smiled sweetly at him. "And besides, that pathetic display of frat-boy egotism never did work on me."

"Pathetic?" the guard growled as he shoved his card back in his pocket. "You're a little bitch, aren't you? I think it's time you took your friend here and left before I throw you off the property."

"Go ahead and try it," Joy challenged, her patience completely gone. "I'll have you arrested for assault and battery, and then I'm quite certain Ms. Preston will have you blacklisted from your security job."

"No one threatens me, you little—"

"I think you better step back, Gary," Curls said from behind him. "Ms. Preston is eager to speak with them."

Baldy scowled but did as his partner said. He narrowed his eyes at Joy. "You better watch yourself. Just because you're a friend of the movie star, it doesn't mean you're hot shit." He looked her up and down. "In fact, you're not hot at all. There's not much to work with, is there, Mikey?"

Mikey cleared his throat and shrugged as he shoved his hands in his pockets, clearly uncomfortable.

"Listen you little toad—" Hope started.

Joy grabbed Hope's hand and tugged her toward the front door. Leaning in, she whispered, "Forget about him. He's not important."

"He's a jackass," she said, raising her voice to make sure he could hear her.

"He is, but I don't have the energy for this." Joy really didn't care what Baldy thought of her. She was used to men ogling Hope with an interested eye. She had the classic hourglass shape that seemed to be so pleasing to men and women alike. Meanwhile, Joy was tall and willowy without much shape at all. She didn't have any body issues. She knew she was pretty in a classical sense; she just didn't have the type of body that Hope had.

"Right," Hope said. "But if I run into him again, he's going to get junk-punched."

Joy snickered. "I hope I'm there to witness it when his eyes roll to the back of his head and he looks like he's going to vomit."

"Well, that vision certainly cheered me up," Hope said with a laugh.

Joy knocked on the door.

A few seconds later, the door cracked open, and Carly, who was hiding behind it, said, "Hurry and get in here before the cameras go off."

"Too late," Joy said. They'd been snapping ever since she and Hope arrived. The pair walked in, and Carly quickly shut the door. "I won't be surprised to see Hope and me on the front page of the gossip rag tomorrow."

Carly grimaced. "I'm sorry you had to deal with that."

Joy waved an unconcerned hand. "Don't worry about any of that. We have more important matters to discuss."

"Let's go in the other room." Carly led them into her expansive kitchen and waved at the breakfast table. "Have a seat. I'll get you something to drink."

"Carly," Joy said. "I had another vision."

She froze. Then she slowly turned back around, her eyes wide. "About Harlow?"

Joy nodded. "I saw where she is."

"Where?" Carly rushed over to her and clutched her arm. "We need to go get her."

"I don't know where exactly. I just saw the room she's being held in."

Hope moved into the kitchen, and just as she had earlier that morning, she put herself to work making coffee.

Carly slumped down into one of the chairs. "You have no idea at all where?"

Joy shook her head and sat next to her. She described the room overlooking the lush rose garden.

"Princess pink?" Carly asked, her brow furrowing.

"It was over the top, but high end. Wherever she is, there is money involved."

Carly was silent for a long moment. Then she muttered, "Shit."

Joy had the distinct impression that Carly had an idea of who might have snatched her niece. "I'm sorry I don't have more information, but I thought you should know." Hope placed a mug in front of Carly and raised an eyebrow at Joy, silently asking if she wanted anything. Joy shook her head. "We should probably go. I still need to swing by the police station and let them know about my vision."

Carly grasped Joy's wrist, stopping her from leaving the table. "No. You can't do that."

"What? Why?"

She carefully let go of Joy's wrist and sat back with a concerned expression on her face. "I just don't want you to get held up at the police station again. Last time it took me hours to get you sprung from their interrogation. And I don't know how much this information will help them."

"I certainly can't get stuck there. I need to be on set this afternoon," Joy said. Then she peered at Carly. "But don't you think it's better if the police know? I know it's not a lot, but it could help."

Carly shook her head. "No. I have a private detective looking into who might've done this. I'll let him know these knew details. If he gets any leads, we'll tell the investigator then."

Private investigator? Joy didn't know what to make of that. Did that mean Carly didn't have any faith in the police investigators? Or was she just using every available resource to find her niece? Yes, that must've been it. Carly had resources Joy could only dream about. Joy was certain that if she were in the same position, if the person missing were one of her kids, she'd do the same. "Okay. That's probably a good idea."

"It is," Carly said reassuringly. She stood and grabbed the phone that was lying on the counter. She turned it on and grimaced. "Mailbox full."

Joy nodded. "Yep. I tried to call before we came over."

She gritted her teeth, initiated her call, and then waited. Finally she said, "I have information that might help."

Joy listened as Carly relayed the details of the room and the garden. Then Carly lowered her voice and exited the room.

Hope moved and sat next to Joy. "That was a little weird, don't you think?"

"A little." She looked at her friend. "Did you pick up anything from the brain waves?"

Chuckling, she shook her head. "No. Want me to try?"

"No," Joy said. "I know it's your new superpower, but I

don't really feel right about intentionally invading someone's privacy."

"Couldn't agree more."

When Carly returned to the kitchen, she said, "Thanks for the information. I'll let you know if my guy finds anything." Then she stuffed a picture frame into Joy's hands. "It's Harlow. I thought you should take it with you. Maybe if you could periodically try to see if you can access any other visions?"

Joy bit her bottom lip. If she never had another vision, it would be too soon for her. After passing out earlier, she wasn't too keen to repeat the experience. Still, she accepted the photo and told Carly she'd try.

"Thank you," the other actress said, her eyes glistening with tears. "Your help means the world to me."

Joy stood and wrapped her in a hug. "There's nothing to thank me for. I just want her home safe."

Carly walked them to the front door. Before she could open it, Hope said, "Baldy is planning to sell a story to the newspapers."

"What story?" Carly asked.

"I don't know for sure. Something about the guy Harlow's been dating. Quinton somebody."

"Dammit, how did he know that?" Carly asked.

Hope shrugged. "No idea."

Her back stiffened, and Carly narrowed her eyes and peered at Hope. "And how do *you* know he wants to sell that story?"

"Hope can sometimes read thoughts," Joy said. "It's not intentional. It just happens."

"Seriously?" Carly glanced between them. "You two are like characters straight out of that television show *Heroes*. The only question is, do you use your powers for good or evil?"

Joy was certain she'd meant for her tone to be light and joking, but it came out strained, as if she were nervous or worried about something.

"Only good. I promise," Hope said with an easy smile. Only her voice was a smidge too high and her smile a little too wide, and Joy could tell it was forced.

Carly didn't seem to notice, though, because she just nodded absently and said, "That's good."

"I need to get to the set," Joy said, suddenly anxious to get out of there. She could just feel it in her bones that Carly was hiding something from them, and Joy was too tired to deal with it anymore.

"Right." Carly gave her a grateful smile. "They gave me until Monday. I just hope we find Harlow by them."

Joy reached out and squeezed her hand. "So do I."

CHAPTER SEVEN

"*A*re you all right?" Hope asked Joy as she stopped her SUV outside of the filming location.

Joy shook her head. "Not really. All I want to do is go home and watch over Kyle. But I'm here and have to film a scene with my least favorite person on the planet."

"It's only supposed to take a few hours, right?"

"Hopefully." Joy sucked in a breath and let it out in a long sigh. "It depends on how the princess is behaving."

"Don't worry about a thing. I'm headed back to your house. I'll make sure Kyle is doing all right. I'll even cook your dinner. Just give me a text when you're ready for me to come pick you up."

Joy reached over and hugged her friend. "You're the best."

"I know." Hope winked at her.

"Love you."

"Love you, too, movie star."

Joy rolled her eyes, but some of the ache in her chest had lessened, and she took a moment to send a thank you to the gods for blessing her with the best friends a girl could ever have.

* * *

"I⊤'s about time you showed up," Prissy said, scowling at Joy when she walked into the makeup tent.

Joy didn't even bother acknowledging the younger actress. She really was well and truly over her.

Prissy sneered in her direction when she realized that Joy wasn't going to play her game. Then she pasted on a soft smile and let worry seep into her eyes before speaking in an overly concerned tone. "What happened to your face? Poor Sam is going to have a hell of a time covering those unfortunate blemishes."

"Oh, hell," Joy muttered and couldn't keep herself from glancing in the mirror of Sam's makeup station. What she saw looking back at her honestly made her want to cry. She was a forty-eight-year-old woman who hadn't had an acne problem since she was fifteen. And suddenly, when she was sure to be in the papers and had a movie to film, she had not just the two blemishes she'd had the day before, but two more had popped up as well.

"Joy, do you think you're having a reaction to the makeup?" Sam asked, the concern in her tone obviously authentic as she studied Joy's face. "If it's going to happen, it usually presents itself right away, but it's not unheard of for actors to start developing sensitivities to certain brands."

"I have no idea. I've had a stressful few days, but honestly, I've never had this reaction to stress before, so I don't know." She sat back in the chair and closed her eyes. Exhaustion washed over her, and she wished with everything she had that she could just go home and fall into bed.

"I bet it's her diet," Prissy said gleefully as she clasped her hands together. "I've heard fried food can do that to a person."

"I don't eat fried food," Joy said wearily.

"Oh? My mistake. I thought since you had those extra pounds that you were one of those all-you-can-eat seafood platter lovers."

"Oh, for the love of Peter, Paul, and Mary!" Joy jerked upright in her chair. "Just stop talking, Prissy. No one wants to hear it."

Prissy narrowed her eyes and moved closer to Joy. In a low, warning voice she said, "Careful, Joy. In addition to your bad skincare, you'll develop a reputation for being hard to work with. You don't want that, do you?"

Anger coiled in Joy's gut, and it was if the dam of emotion she'd been holding back the past twenty-four hours shattered, and all of her restraint vanished. "Oh, shut up, you hateful bitch!"

There was silence in the tent as Prissy and Sam stared at her opened mouthed. Then Sam let out a loud snicker before clasping her hand over her mouth, trying to stifle it. Prissy turned her scathing glare on the makeup artist and said, "You'll be lucky if you aren't fired by the time the evening is over."

"Just let it go," Joy said, tiredly. "This is between you—"

"Do. Not. Talk. To. Me," the actress spit out, her face so red the color clashed with her orange blouse.

"I see. So it's okay for you to antagonize Sam and me, but neither of us are allowed to call you on it?" Joy shook her head. "You need to grow up, Prissy."

"Grow up?" she said incredulously. "A forty-eight-year-old

newbie to the industry is telling me to grow up? How *dare* you?"

Joy opened her mouth to defend herself, but Prissy threw her hands up in the air, stomped her foot, and yelled, "Finn, I can't work under these conditions. Let's see if the know-it-all can do the damned scene by herself!"

She spun on her heel and stalked out of the tent.

Joy and Sam moved to the door of the tent and watched Prissy arguing with the director before she hurried off to the small adjacent parking lot.

"Oh, no." Joy sighed as Finn Chance glared in the direction of the tent.

Scowling, he hurried toward Joy and erupted with a loud, "Joy! What the fuck?"

Joy winced and cowered back into the tent even though he had obviously already spotted her.

He tore into the tent, ranting about losing money and he should've known better than to cast someone with no experience. "Where's the professionalism? How the hell are we going to meet our budget and timeline if no one is here to film?"

"I know you're upset," Joy said calmly. "But I would like to point out that I'm the only one who is here and ready to work."

He stopped pacing and stared at her. Finn Chance was a tall man with a full head of black curly hair. Normally his blue eyes were the color of the ocean, but today they were dull gray and full of impatience. "Do you think I'm blind? Obviously, you're here. But our main star just walked out because you two can't get along. Fix it. Or else I'll recast you."

Joy gaped at him. "Recast me? But we've already filmed half the movie!"

"Don't test me," he warned. "There are hundreds of

actresses in your age range who will do this for far less than we're paying you. The only reason you got this job is because the perfume campaign went viral. But don't think that kind of hype lasts forever. Get it together and get Prissy back here first thing Monday, or you're out."

"Yeah. Sure," Joy said, agreeing. She knew what to do to calm Prissy down. It involved groveling and coercing Joy's non-boyfriend into going to Prissy's cocktail party, but she could do it. The thought of kowtowing to the director in front of her after he berated *her* for Prissy's bad behavior was infuriating. The fact was, acting had always been a dream of hers, and she'd be damned if she'd let Finn Chance or Prissy Penderton take it away from her. "We'll be here Monday."

"Make sure you are." He started to leave but then glanced back and added, "And do something about your face."

Joy stood there stunned as she watched him go.

As soon as he was out of earshot, Sam hissed, "Bastard."

"I was going to go with something a little stronger, but that works." Joy closed her eyes and tried to push aside the crushing self-doubt. She worked up her courage and looked at Sam and her perfect creamy skin. "I have no idea why this is happening, but do you have any suggestions on how to clear it up?"

"Come with me." Sam led Joy over to her station. "I have an herbal mixture that should do the trick. All it takes is twenty-four hours."

"Let's do it."

An hour later, with her face tingling more than was comfortable, Joy called Hope and asked her to pick her up in a half hour. Then she took off to the beach, in desperate need of some water therapy.

The wind whipped off the California coast, blowing her long blond hair behind her as she walked along the shore.

Images of Harlow flashed in her mind, and she couldn't help the crushing worry for the young woman she hadn't even had the opportunity to meet. Suddenly her problems with the movie director seemed insignificant.

She stopped near a large rock outcropping and stared out at the horizon. Normally the sea energized her. It filled her up and helped center her so that she felt confident in her life choices. But in that moment, she was completely unsettled. Her new career wasn't everything she'd dreamed. She was single now; separated from the man who'd emotionally left her years ago. She'd imagined herself dating, having a hot affair or two, and then maybe finding someone else to settle down with. Maybe that was all Troy was—a hot affair. Wasn't it better to not have any expectations from the man who hadn't called her in weeks?

If it were up to her, she'd write him off completely. But now she needed to make Prissy happy, so that she'd make their director happy. Even though Joy wasn't sure she wanted to keep acting, she absolutely wanted to finish the movie and give it everything she had. If it didn't work out or she decided it wasn't for her, she could always go back to her position as vice president of the Arts Market. Technically, she was still the vice president, but she'd taken a leave to make the movie. Or maybe she could open an art gallery. Premonition Pointe was growing, and she'd considered opening a handmade gallery before.

"This doesn't have to be forever. Neither does Troy." Just saying the words out loud settled some of the turmoil spiraling through her. The most important things in her life weren't things at all. People were important, specifically her kids and her coven and now Carly and her niece. Since the vision, she'd felt a connection to Harlow that wasn't going away.

Joy took a deep breath and let out all the anxiety that had coiled in her gut, and suddenly she felt comfortable in her own skin again. She smiled to herself. The sea never let her down. She walked back up to the parking lot and pulled her phone out. She scrolled through her contacts until she found the one she was looking for and then hit Call.

On the third ring, Troy picked up. "Well hello there, gorgeous. I was wondering when I'd hear from you."

Joy frowned. "Oh? You were waiting for *me* to call *you*?"

"Sure. Why not?"

Why not indeed? "I guess I just figured you'd call when you were done with your project. I didn't want to bother you."

He chuckled. "I'm never too busy for a gorgeous woman."

Something about the way he'd said those words made her stomach sour. Had he been hooking up with models the whole time he'd been gone? She imagined he had. Why wouldn't he? They weren't dating. They hadn't made any promises. He was free to do whatever he wanted.

"Joy? Are you still there?" he asked.

She cleared her throat. "Yeah. I'm here. Listen, I read that you'll be in town this weekend, and I was wondering if you could do me a huge favor."

"What is it?" he asked, sounding more than a little wary.

Joy didn't waste time on preamble; she just let it fly. "Prissy Penderton has been harassing me about bringing you to her cocktail party on Saturday night. Apparently, the gossip rags have convinced her we are a couple. And while I was going to blow her off, I now have to make nice with her because there is tension on the set." She grimaced at the way that sounded. "I'm sorry. I know that sounds like I'm using you. You don't have to do this. I can find—"

"I'll be there," he said, cutting her off. "What time do you want me to pick you up?"

"Um, are you sure?" she asked, flustered. She really hadn't been expecting him to be so willing to go with her to a spoiled actress's party.

"I'm sure. Is seven okay? The gallery showing is until five."

"Seven is perfect." She smiled, feeling like something had finally gone right. "But I'll see you before then. I can't miss your show."

He was quiet for a moment, and then he said, "I'd like that."

Her earlier feelings of unease had completely vanished, and she ended the call feeling lighter than she had in weeks.

CHAPTER EIGHT

"*H*e's fine," Hope stressed, leading the way to the bluff overlooking the ocean.

"He didn't sound fine," Joy said, still uneasy about leaving Kyle by himself. When she'd gotten home from the beach, he'd been upright on his crutches, hobbling into the kitchen for some water.

At first, she'd been happy to see him up and around, but when she'd taken a good look at him, she noted that he was so pale he looked like he hadn't seen the sun in weeks, and he'd had a sheen of sweat on his skin. She'd tried to force him back to bed with hot tea and a cool towel to mop up his skin. But he'd waved her off and insisted he was fine. That he couldn't stay in bed for the rest of his life and that she should go out. He could take care of himself.

Joy had her doubts, but even though it killed her to leave, she'd respected his wishes. He was a grown man after all. Hovering and acting like he was dying was only going to send him back to his second-floor apartment, and that was something she couldn't let him do. Not until he could walk again. Or at least when he was stronger.

"Yes, he did," Hope said. "He just needed to hydrate and clean up. You'll see when I take you home. He'll be on the couch with the remote and your bag of salt and vinegar potato chips."

"For once, I'd be happy to let him have my chips," Joy said.

Hope laughed. "So that's what it takes for you to share? A broken leg?"

Joy chuckled. "I guess we found my breaking point."

The pair were still chuckling when they found Gigi and Grace sitting on a blanket surrounded by a large circle of flickering candles.

"Did you start without us?" Joy asked, taking in her other two coven mates. Grace had lost her shimmering blue suit and was now dressed in jeans and a formfitting T-shirt. Gigi, the newest member of their coven, was wearing black leggings and a flowy deep-purple top that was cinched at the waist.

"We only put out the candles," Grace said, getting to her feet and hugging Joy. "We still need to uncork the wine."

"I'm on it!" Gigi held two bottles up and grinned, her amber eyes glinting from the moonlight.

"Make mine a double." Joy sighed as she sat next to Gigi and immediately found herself engulfed in another hug. The movement took her by surprise. Gigi wasn't exactly the most touchy-feely witch in the world. Or at least she hadn't been before, but maybe she was making up for it now that she'd joined their coven.

"How are you doing?" Gigi asked her. "Grace filled me in on everything. It's a lot to deal with."

"It is. But I don't want to make this all about me. Kyle is going to be okay. He's just out of commission for a bit. It's really Harlow and Carly I'm worried about. I just wish I could do more for them."

"That's why we're here," Grace said, lifting her tote bag in the air for everyone to see. "And that's why I brought supplies. We just need to decide which spell to try first."

Joy raised an eyebrow at her friend. "Have you been researching spells, Grace?"

Grace grinned. "Why yes, I have. In fact, I spent all afternoon pouring over my books. After my showing today, I needed to do something to occupy my mind. Otherwise, I was going to pace and stare at the phone for hours, mentally willing my client to make an offer."

"How did it go? Was he interested?" Gigi asked. "I can't imagine he isn't. That place is gorgeous. If I'd had that kind of budget, I wouldn't have hesitated." Gigi had recently moved to Premonition Pointe and had purchased a lovely, albeit haunted, home right on the beach. It wasn't a compound with its own private beach, however.

"I could see you there," Grace said with a kind smile. "It's classic and yet, otherworldly, just like you."

"That's... really kind of you to say," Gigi said, glancing away and looking a bit shy.

That's new, Joy thought. Gigi wasn't exactly a shy woman. She had a backbone of steel that had helped her bring down her abusive ex-husband.

"Anyway," Grace said. "I just couldn't get a read on the guy. I think he liked it. He spent a long time checking the place out, kicking the tires and looking under the hood, but he didn't give me any indication of his intentions. I'll just have to wait and see what he does."

As Joy sat and listened to Grace describe her favorite parts of the house, she watched her. Grace had divorced recently, started a new job, and even had a younger boyfriend who was just perfect for her. She'd always been a strong, capable woman even before her husband left her for the office receptionist, but after she'd been on her own, she'd really blossomed. Now she was everything Joy always wanted to be—successful, independent, content, and in love with a man who adored her. Joy could have that, too, right?

Of course she could. Though she had a hard time seeing Troy as her love-interest. She needed more commitment and stability than he could offer. Didn't she?

Joy shook her head. This wasn't the time to be contemplating her life choices. They needed to find Harlow.

When Grace finally sighed and took a long sip of the red wine Gigi had handed her, Joy leaned forward and asked, "Are you going to teach us the finding spell we're going use on Harlow, or were you hoping we'd all fall so hopelessly in love with the Emsworth estate that we'd all pool our money and form a commune?"

"Very funny." Grace rolled her eyes. Then she raised her eyebrows and asked, "Do you think that's an option? I'm down for a shared real estate investment."

"Good try, Gracie," Hope said, chuckling. "But unless we figure out how to conjure money, I think we're SOL."

"It's a nice dream." Grace took another long swig of wine. "Fine. We'll leave the daydreaming for another time. Let's get down to business."

Joy shifted anxiously. Normally, she loved the meetings with her coven on the bluff. But they very rarely did spells that were so important, and they were never a matter of life and death. Usually they did intention spells or glamour spells or blessings. Not finding spells, which normally were rife with ethical issues. It wasn't that she felt any sort of remorse for searching out Harlow's abductor, but the spell was new and powerful, and it was making her uneasy not knowing what might come of it.

"Joy, do you have the picture?" Grace asked.

Joy nodded and reached into her tote bag for the framed photo Carly had given her.

"Perfect." Grace whipped out a velvet cloth that had a pentagram embroidered on it and placed the cloth in the middle of the circle. Then she placed the photo in the very center of the pentagram. "That should do. Are we ready?"

Gigi and Hope nodded.

"Wait." Joy frowned at them, her body rigid with agitation. "We don't even know what we're doing."

Hope had an easy smile as she shrugged. "I trust Grace."

Rolling her eyes, Joy said, "Obviously, I trust her, too. But I just feel unprepared. Don't you think we should be prepared for something this big? I just think we need to go into this spell with intention and precision."

"Good point," Gigi said quietly as she squeezed Joy's hand. "Maybe we can run through it first?"

"Uh, sure." Grace said, her eyebrows furrowed. Her enthusiasm had vanished, and she gave Joy a strange look as she added, "Sorry about that. I was just going to lead the spell and got carried away, I guess."

Everyone was silent, and the energy between them was awkward and strange. It wasn't something Joy was used to. Normally the group just clicked. These women were her sisters and the people she trusted most in the world. *Dammit.* Stress had gotten the better of her.

"No, you didn't," Joy said, trying to fight the bone-deep weariness that she knew was making her testy. "I'm just not firing on all cylinders and am being difficult. Sorry."

Grace's expression immediately changed to one of understanding. "It's all right, honey. Don't worry about it another second. Here." She handed Joy the spell she'd handwritten on a piece of paper. "Since the spell is centered on you, I think you're probably the one who needs to internalize it."

Joy scanned the spell and let out a gasp. "I'm going to be the vessel for finding Harlow?"

"Sure. You're the one who sees visions of her," Grace said, giving her a bright smile. "The spell is for a seer, so I figured that's you."

"I'm not a seer," Joy said quietly. But was she? She'd had two visions in less than twenty-four hours.

"You are now, sweetie," Grace said. "Now get comfy with the spell, because I'm feeling extra witchy today."

"Extra witchy? What the hell does that mean?" Hope asked with a laugh. "You're not planning on making a potion with eye of newt and the toenails of your enemy, are you?"

"No toenails. There's no way I'm going near Bill's feet again," she said, referring to her ex-husband.

"Is he really your enemy?" Hope asked, her face alight with humor. "I would've thought that would be Shondra Barns, the backstabbing receptionist who slept with him."

Grace seemed to contemplate her question for a moment and then shrugged. "Either way. I'm not touching her toenails either. There's no telling what kind of fungus she's walking around with."

Joy couldn't help it. She let out a bark of laughter. "You two are ridiculous."

They both grinned. Hope raised her palm to Grace, and as they high-fived, she said, "Mission accomplished."

Gigi shook her head and chuckled. "One of these days I'm

going to know all of these stories and be right in the thick of things."

"We know. That's why we coerced you into our circle of doom," Grace said and filled her empty glass with wine.

Gigi grinned, raised her glass in toast, and said, "To the circle of doom."

Joy, Hope, and Grace cheerfully joined in her toast, and once they drained their glasses, Joy glanced at her friends and was once again overwhelmed by how lucky she was to have their support. "Okay," Joy said. "Grace? Are you ready to lead this spell?"

"I'm ready if you are," Grace said, all traces of the earlier tension gone.

"Ready." Joy passed the handwritten spell back to Grace and stood. "I assume this spell requires us to be upright?"

Grace nodded and gestured for the other two women to get to their feet. The moment they were standing, Grace raised her arms high in the air, waited for magic to appear at her fingertips, and then swung her arms down quickly as she said, "Let the night bathe us in moonlight."

The candles went out instantly, and the silver moonlight illuminated the picture lying in the middle of the circle.

Grace grinned, clearly pleased that the spell had started out strong. But her smile quickly vanished, and Grace held her hands out to the side, nodding for them to do the same. They each grabbed hands, forming a circle. "From earth and sky and fire and sea, we call the goddess of the moon. Hear our call and help us find the one we seek."

The candles flared to life again, illuminating the small circle.

"Joy, move into the middle of the circle and hold Harlow's picture in your hands," Grace commanded.

Magic strummed through Joy, filling her up and making her feel as if anything was possible. She released her sisters' hands and stepped forward into the pentagram, and without even realizing she'd reached for the picture, she found the photo of Harlow in her hands. Her coven members closed ranks around her, clasping hands again, and the magic filling the air was so vibrant, Joy felt almost as if she were floating.

"Goddess of the moon, shine your light, bless Joy with the sight," Grace called.

The other two joined in as they chanted the intention.

Joy held the photo up to the moon and just like that, images of a large white Victorian home bathed in a swath of sunlight filled her mind. The front lawn was immaculate and had a long pathway framed by colorful mums and pansies. There was a row of cherry trees lining the property on one side while the other was bordered by forest land. Joy tried to glance around, looking for an address or street sign, but she had no luck. The house was set back from the road and there was a long dirt driveway.

The vision vanished, and Joy blinked, trying to let her eyes adjust to the darkness again.

Grace placed a soft hand on Joy's arm. "What did you see?"

Joy turned to her, completely disoriented. The vision had been different than the other two she'd experienced. Those had run in her mind sort of like a movie. In this one, she felt like she'd been transported to the white Victorian, only to be immediately relocated back to Premonition Pointe. "Huh?"

"Did you see where Harlow is?" Grace tried again.

"Yes. I think I did," Joy said, finally getting her bearings. "Only, I still have no idea where that is!" The frustration was palpable as she came to understand that the spell had worked.

It just hadn't been specific enough. She peered at Grace. "We need to do it again."

Grace shook her head and bit her bottom lip. "I don't think we can."

"Why not?" Joy glanced at Hope and Gigi and noticed both of them were lying on the blanket. Hope had her arm draped over her eyes while Gigi was staring at the sky, taking deep breaths.

"That was a long time to hold the magic," Grace said as she sank to the blanket. "We're all exhausted."

Confusion made Joy do a double take. What did she mean by that had been a long time to hold their magic? To her if felt as if the entire thing had taken just a few minutes. She studied her coven mates and noted that all three of them had tired eyes and lacked the vibrant energy they'd had before the spell. "How long was I gone?"

Grace pulled her phone out of her pocket and glanced at the time. "Forty minutes."

"Forty minutes! You're kidding me, right?" How was that even possible? "What was I doing that whole time?"

"At first you were just levitating, your eyes wide, but unseeing. I figured you were in another plane, maybe in a vision. But then, finally, you were alert and obviously studying something. It didn't take long before you started mumbling about cherry trees and no address."

"Oh, wow. I had no idea. It felt very quick to me. I don't remember the time when I was unresponsive. Sorry. You three worked hard for the information I did get," Joy said. "I just wish it was more helpful."

Grace gave her a tired smile. "It's all right. Just tell us what you saw, and we'll go from there."

Joy nodded and went through the details of the white

69

Victorian, the cherry trees, the manicured lawn and flowers, the forest, and the fact that the house was set back from the road without a street sign. "That's why I wanted to try again. We need to ask to see the street so we can find that house. It could be anywhere."

"Not just anywhere," Gigi said thoughtfully. "Some of the details will narrow it down, right? Like the forest. We know she's not being held in a city. Then there's the cherry trees. Those don't grow just anywhere."

"Right," Grace added. "And the Victorian. If it's an older turn-of-the-century home and not one built recently in the same style, that helps, too. If you could sketch it out, I could maybe try searching real estate transactions to see if anything comes up."

Joy gave her a look that said she thought her friend had lost her mind. "That seems like a longshot at best."

Grace shrugged. "Maybe, but it's worth a try."

"I agree it's a longshot," Hope said. "I mean what are the chances that house has been on the market recently? But it's something to try when we have very little else to go on."

"All right." Joy rummaged in her handbag and pulled out a small notebook she'd started keeping with her when she became vice president of the Arts Market Co-op. Too many times she'd been caught off guard by running into artists who had something they needed for her to fix. She'd given up on remembering and finally went with the small diary for all their grievances. And there were a lot. In some ways, Joy was glad to have taken a leave of absence from the board. Everyone always wanted something from her. But in other ways, she very much missed the art. It was what had gotten her involved in the first place.

Joy had always been fairly decent at drawing. Especially

architecture. It had been a favorite elective of hers when she'd been getting her theater arts degree in college. But when she'd gotten married and had kids, there just wasn't enough time or energy to devote to either her acting or her love of sketching. Even when she'd gotten involved in the Arts Market, she hadn't put any priority on trying to sell her own drawings. Instead, she'd focused on trying to help other artists market their work. It was satisfying helping people succeed.

She was a little rusty, but it didn't take long to get the house and the grounds down in her sketch book. Joy passed it to Grace. Hope and Gigi immediately moved to studying the drawing over her shoulder. "If I had my colored pencils, I could really make this come to life."

"Damn, Joy," Gigi said, her eyes wide. "You're good."

"Isn't she though?" Hope said with a sigh. "I've been trying to get her to devote time to her drawings for years, but so far she just keeps blowing me off."

"I've been a little busy," Joy said with a shrug, but she couldn't help the smile that claimed her lips at the praise.

"Can you do me a favor?" Grace asked Joy as she eyed the drawing.

"Of course," Joy said automatically. "Anything."

"Color this in and then send me a picture of it." She finally took her eyes off the drawing. "That will help when I try to find recent real estate transactions. I might be able to load it into Google and do a reverse image search."

Joy's skepticism for the plan started to fade. If there was a way the computer could help with the match, it just might work. But then she frowned. "Like we were talking about earlier, this sounds like a longshot at best. Do you have any reason to believe this property would come up in the records?"

"No. Not really," Grace said, pursing her lips. "But it's

something. And if we do get a hit, that's worth all the effort. If we don't? All we've wasted is some time."

"It's a decent idea," Gigi said.

"I'm all for it then." Joy smiled at them, feeling a little better that they at least had some sort of plan going forward.

Hope nodded her agreement. "And while Grace is working on that, I'm going to ask Angela to keep a mental ear out just in case Harlow's abductor is hanging around town."

"You really don't need to do that," Joy said automatically and then wanted to kick herself. Why was she discouraging help they obviously needed? "I just mean that I know how much of a toll it takes on her, and I don't want her to have to go through all of that."

"We'll leave it up to her," Hope said firmly. "But I'm willing to bet we won't be able to keep her away from the Bird's Eye Bakery. I know her. She'll want to do anything she can to help. She might not like spending a lot of time with people, but she has a kind heart. It would really bother her to not do everything she could to find Harlow."

"Okay," Joy said, unable to work up the energy to argue further. Then she smiled. "Thank you."

"I just wish there was more we could do," Grace said.

"You've already done more than expected." Joy laid down on the blanket and stared up at the stars. The cool breeze off the ocean made gooseflesh pop up on her arms, and she shivered. But she wasn't cold. She was just happy to feel something other than dread. She closed her eyes and just listened to the sound of the waves crashing below.

"Joy?" Hope called.

"What?" Joy asked without opening her eyes.

"Are you sleeping out here tonight?"

Joy's eyes popped open, and she looked up at her friends.

They'd already packed everything up except the blanket she was lying on. Had she fallen asleep and not noticed? Was she in a weird magical time warp? She needed to get home before she slipped into an entirely different reality. "No. I need to go check on Kyle."

Hope held out a hand to help her up and asked, "Are you all right? You look disoriented."

Joy ran a hand down her face. "I'm just exhausted."

Gigi appeared beside Joy and slipped an arm through hers. "We've got you. Come on."

The four of them made their way back to the road where they deposited Joy into Hope's SUV.

"Thanks again," Joy told them as she buckled her seatbelt.

"No worries." Grace leaned in and kissed her on the cheek.

When it was Gigi's turn, she tucked a small jar into Joy's hand and whispered, "Thought you could use this. I always break out when I'm stressed, and this salve clears everything right up."

Joy blinked and looked down at the jar. There wasn't any label. "Did you make this?"

She grinned. "Yes. I have a knack for herbs. Just dab a little on problem areas before you go to bed and tomorrow morning, your skin will be totally clear."

"Thank you." Joy reached over and gave her a hug. "You're the best." Joy thought back to earlier in the day when Sam had given her a facial and an ointment and then frowned when it didn't make an immediate difference. Sam told her to call if nothing changed within twenty-four hours. Maybe Gigi's cream was the magic she needed.

"Let's fly," Hope said, jumping into the SUV.

Joy nodded, and before Hope even pulled out onto the road, Joy leaned her head against the window and fell fast asleep.

CHAPTER NINE

"*W*ake up, Sleeping Beauty."

Joy jerked awake. She glanced around and groaned when a pain shot up her neck. She reached up, massaging the kink out of her sore muscles. "Oh, good goddess. I am feeling every one of my forty-eight years."

"Been there." Hope smiled sympathetically. "Need help getting inside? Maybe a wheelchair or a walker?"

"You're evil," Joy said without any heat. Then she laughed. "I feel like I could sleep for a week." She peered at her friend, who'd been driving her around all day. "How is it that you aren't dead on your feet? You've been babysitting me all day."

"I'm just better at faking it." Hope winked at her but then turned serious. "Are you really okay? Do you need me to do anything before I go?"

Joy shook her head as a rush of love washed over her. "No. Thank you, but I'm going to go in there, color my drawing, and send it to both Grace and Carly. Then I'm climbing into the bath before I crawl into bed and sleep for twelve hours."

"That sounds heavenly," Hope said with a sigh.

"Not as heavenly as cuddling up with a sexy dark-haired man who can't keep his hands off you," Joy said, referring to Hope's fiancé, Lucas.

"Well, I can't complain about that, but every now and then I crave a little me time. If I were to sink into a bath, he'd probably crawl in after me and then forget relaxing. The man is insatiable."

"Stop. Now you're just bragging," Joy said as she climbed out of the SUV. "Go home. Have fun. I'll call you tomorrow."

"Love you," Hope called.

"Love you, too." Joy waved and quickly made her way up the walk to her front door.

The house was dark when Joy entered. She turned the light on and glanced around. There had been a time when her home had been her sanctuary. It was where she was most content and at one time, she'd thought she'd never leave. But now that Paul was gone and her kids had moved on, it just felt overwhelming. Sure, Kyle was back for a short time, but that was temporary. He'd leave again soon, and then she'd be rambling around in a large four-bedroom home full of some of her best memories, but also some of her worst.

She sighed, locked the front door, and went to the kitchen to get some water. Maybe she should talk to Grace about moving. Maybe she'd get a smaller, cozier place right on the beach… if she could afford it.

After draining her glass, she put the few dishes that were in the sink into the dishwasher, wiped the counters down, and locked the back door before heading down the hall to check on Kyle. But when she got to his room, the door was open and his bed was empty.

Her heart started to race. Where was he? Not in the living room and not the kitchen. She'd just been there. Panic started to take over and she imagined him sprawled on the floor somewhere, unable to haul himself back up because he broke something else or further injured his leg. She quickly moved down the hall to check the bathroom.

Empty.

An ache formed in her stomach. Where was he?

Joy hurried from room to room, only to find the entire house empty. There was only one place left to look. She turned down the hallway that led to her bedroom and let out a sigh of relief when she saw the light streaming from her room.

"Kyle?" she called as she walked into her room.

He didn't respond.

Her panic started to mount again until she saw the light shining under the door of her bathroom. She frowned. What was he doing in there?

She moved across the room and was about to knock when she heard a distinctly male grunt followed by Kyle's voice. "Careful. You're manhandling precious cargo."

"Shut up, or I won't finish you off," came a second male voice.

Joy froze as the sound of laughter filtered through the door, followed by the distinct sound of water splashing.

Oh, hell, she thought. Her son was taking a bath with another man in her oversized jacuzzi tub. But with who? Jackson? It had to be Jackson.

She started to move away but froze again when she heard a moan. One that was going to be burned in her brain forever. All she'd wanted to do was take a bath and then crawl into bed. Now she was standing in her room listening to her son... do things she should never ever hear.

Joy's flight instinct finally kicked in, and she rushed out of her room and back into the kitchen, where she sat down at the table, put her AirPods in her ears, and started her favorite playlist. Pharrell Williams started singing about being Happy while she went to work on coloring in the drawing she'd made out on the bluff.

A half hour later, with her drawing vibrant with color, she texted it to Grace and then called Carly, praying it didn't head straight to voicemail.

Joy was surprised when Carly answered on the first ring. Joy said, "Hey. I honestly didn't think I was going to get you on the phone."

"I set your number to important so I wouldn't miss your calls," Carly said, her voice sounding tired. "I wanted to be available if you had another vision."

"That was smart thinking." Joy hadn't even known that was an option on the phone.

"Did you see Harlow again?" she asked. There was profound sadness in her tone that made Joy want to cry.

"No. I didn't see Harlow, but my coven helped me do a finding spell, and I saw the house."

Carly sucked in a sharp breath. "You know where she is?" she asked in a low whisper.

Joy hated to disappoint her, but there was no getting around it. "I'm sorry, Carly. I saw the house, but unfortunately, I have no idea where it is. The street name wasn't visible, and I couldn't even see a house number."

"Oh. Well, I'm not sure how that helps, but thanks for—"

"I have a drawing of it," Joy said, cutting her off. "I was going to text it to you in case it's familiar or you want to give it to your private detective."

"Really? Well, it's a step in the right direction, I guess. Thank you. Hopefully he can do something with it. I'll send it over to him ASAP."

"Sure. And I'll make a copy and drop it off with Detective Coolidge tomorrow," Joy said.

"What? No, I can't let you do that," she rushed out. "You've done so much already. I'll take care of it."

Joy actually found herself slumping with relief. She'd been going nonstop for days and was ready to let go of everything. "That would be great. Tell the detective to call me if she has questions."

"I will. Thanks, Joy."

"You're welcome. You know I'd do anything to help. I'm praying Harlow comes home soon."

"Thanks." The line went dead, and Joy sent the text. Then she folded her arms on the table and put her head down for just a moment.

"Mrs. Lansing?"

The familiar voice jerked her awake, and she quickly sat up. Pain shot down her neck again and she cried out, "Ow!"

"Whoa, are you okay?" Jackson sat in the chair next to her and reached out as if he was going to massage her neck but then dropped his hand at the last moment.

"Yeah. I'm okay. I guess I fell asleep, and now my neck has seized up. A bath—uh, ibuprofen should help."

He glanced down the hall toward Kyle's bedroom. "How long have you been here?"

She shrugged one shoulder. "Not sure. Forty-five minutes or so."

Silence fell between them until he cleared his throat. "I came over to give Kyle a hand."

"Sure." She glanced away and felt like an idiot that she couldn't look Jackson in the eye. There were just some things mothers shouldn't know. "How is he?"

"Better now that he's had a bath," Jackson said. Then he

laughed and looked down at his shirt. "I guess he managed to give me one, too. It was a little perilous getting him out of your tub. It's so deep. But the shower in the hall bath was out of the question because of his cast, so he asked me to help him in and out of the tub. Can't say that's something I thought I'd be doing, but when your... um, friend, needs help, you do what you gotta do, right?"

"You're rambling," Kyle said from the doorway of the kitchen. He was propped up on his crutches, his face freshly scrubbed and his hair still wet.

Joy glanced between them and didn't miss the panicked look on Jackson's face. Although, curiously, Kyle just looked amused. Joy rose from her chair and walked over to her son. She placed her palms on his cheeks and asked, "How are you doing, really?"

He smiled at her, and she was pleased to see it was his easy smile, like he was relaxed and not in constant pain. "Better. Can we go sit in the living room? I think we need to talk."

"Sure, baby. Do you want anything? Water? Tea? Coffee?" Joy reached for the kettle, intending to make herself a cup of tea.

"Water for me," Kyle said. "Jackson will have tea. Herbal, no caffeine."

"Hey! What if I want caffeine?" Jackson protested.

"It will keep you up all night and then you'll be falling asleep at the espresso machine tomorrow," Kyle said easily. "It's either herbal or decaf for you."

Jackson rolled his eyes, but his lips were curved into a tiny smile. "Herbal, I guess."

"I'm on it," Joy said, happily. "Jackson, help Kyle to the living room. I'll be right out."

Kyle shook his head. "I don't need help to go twenty feet, Mom."

"Just let your boyfriend help you, honey," she said and reached for the tea box. Silence filled the room, and it took her a moment to realize what she'd done. Joy dropped the tea tin on the counter and spun around, horrified at her slip. She'd been waiting for him to tell her when he was ready. "I'm sorry. I shouldn't have said that. I'm tired and it just slipped out."

Kyle and Jackson shared a long look. Then Kyle held his hand out to Jackson. Jackson bit his lower lip but moved to stand next to him and take his hand.

Joy felt tears sting her eyes, and she smiled at them tenderly. "I love you both. You know that, right?"

Kyle nodded.

Jackson swallowed hard. "Thanks, Mrs. Lansing."

"Stop that Mrs. Lansing crap right now, Jackson. Haven't I already told you to call me Joy a hundred times? You're family for god's sake. There's no need for formalities here. Now go into the living room and I'll bring the tea and water in a moment."

Jackson let go of Kyle's hand and watched him for a moment as he crutched his way to the couch. Then he turned to Joy, strode over, and gave her a tight hug. Joy wrapped her arms around the young man who'd been in her son's life since childhood and whispered, "I'm happy for you both."

When Jackson pulled away, he quickly wiped at his eyes and said, "I heard you before at the hospital, but... you know my mom doesn't agree with my 'lifestyle.' And to see how you handled that, well, I'm both very happy and also a little sad because I'll never get something like that from my own mom."

Joy wrapped her arms around Jackson one more time, held him tightly, and said, "You're a treasure, Jackson. Remember that. I'd be proud to be your mother if you weren't dating my son."

He let out a choked laugh and let her go. "That would be creepy, wouldn't it?"

"Just a smidge." She grabbed a glass from the cabinet and handed it to him. "Get Kyle his water while I finish up this tea."

"Yes, ma'am." He winked at her and did as he was told.

A few minutes later, Joy handed Jackson his tea and sat in one of the armchairs across from the couch where the two young men were sitting together. "Okay, here I am. What do we need to talk about?" she asked easily.

"Um…" Kyle cleared his throat. "Well…" He glanced at Jackson, his eyes pleading.

Jackson laughed. "She already knows. Why is it so hard to say it?"

"I don't know," Kyle said hotly. "I've never had to do this before."

"I know." Jackson's expression was tender as he slipped his hand into Kyle's. "But it's already better than the conversation you tried to have with your dad. That's gotta make it easier, right?"

Kyle winced.

"Sorry." Jackson leaned over and gave him a kiss on his cheek.

Joy, who'd been watching their interactions with utter fascination, let out a contented sigh. "You two are adorable. Kyle, why were you never like this with any of your girlfriends?"

Kyle flushed pink.

Jackson's smile widened. "You weren't?"

"Shut up." Kyle punched him lightly on the arm, and Jackson laughed.

Joy laughed too. "Okay, what were you going to tell me? That you're with Jackson? I got that already."

"I'm bi," Kyle said and then stared at her as if waiting for some sort of negative reaction.

Joy frowned. "Okay. I thought that was fairly obvious."

Kyle blinked at her. "You knew?"

"Not until I saw you two together at the hospital. Or rather when I saw Jackson and he was so upset. I guessed then. Surely he told you." Joy nodded to Jackson.

Kyle turned to look at him. "Told me what?"

Jackson winced. "She told me that if we were together, she was fine with it. Then she wouldn't let me say anything at all, insisting that if you wanted to come out it should be when you were ready."

Kyle stared at his boyfriend and then at his mother. "You really said that?" he asked her.

"Of course. You don't think Jackson would lie, do you?"

"He lied by omission. He didn't say a word." He eyed Jackson again. "Hell, Jay, I wouldn't have been nearly as nervous if you'd given me that vital information."

Jackson averted his gaze. "Sorry. I was going to, but then you were in pain and sleeping a lot, and then when I got here, you needed me to help you get a bath and... well, we know how that went."

Kyle snorted. "Yeah. We do."

Joy cleared her throat. "Don't mind me. Just a mother in the room who doesn't need to know what her son does behind closed doors."

"What?" Kyle whipped his head back around, looking at Joy in horror. "Just what do you think went on here tonight?"

Joy held her hands up. "I don't know. Don't want to know."

Jackson threw his head back and laughed.

"Oh. My. God. This conversation is way off the rails," Kyle said. "For the record, I needed someone to help me get into the bath. Balancing on one foot while getting up and down is really hard. Jackson helped me. That's it."

"Well, I also washed your hair and got shampoo in your eye," Jackson said.

"Yeah, thanks for that, by the way. My eye is still irritated."

Jackson shrugged one shoulder. "I kept you from falling and breaking your skull, right?"

"Barely. I do remember falling back into the bath and knocking my elbow."

"And soaking me with bathwater," Jackson added. "It was like a wet T-shirt contest in there for a minute."

Kyle snorted. "I wasn't complaining."

"Okay. Enough," Joy said with a laugh. "I got it. Two boys horsing around in the bath. Apparently, no one has grown up around here."

They both laughed and tilted closer to each other.

When they finally had themselves under control, Joy raised one eyebrow. "Was that it? You're bi and you're dating Jackson?"

"Mostly," Kyle said, sobering.

"Okay," Joy said. "So you're bi. No big deal there. And you're dating Jackson, a young man whom I already love. I don't really see the need for a conversation about this, unless there's something else I need to know."

"Dad was a dick about it," Kyle blurted.

"What?" Joy sat frozen, trying to process the fact that Kyle had told Paul and he'd reacted badly. "When? And what did he say?"

"Right before the accident. I went over there to visit and told him I'm dating Jackson. He just stared at me and then told me to find someone with higher ambitions than working at a café. Preferably a woman so it would be easier for me to start a family."

Joy sat in stunned silence. None of that sounded like Paul. What had he become since they'd separated? "Please tell me you're embellishing what he said."

"Nope. If anything, I'm softening it because I don't want Jackson to know what else he said."

"Kyle," Jackson growled. "You can tell me anything."

"Not if it's going to hurt you needlessly. He was being an elitist bigot. I told him to stick his flank steak up his ass and left."

Joy snorted a laugh. "Did you really?"

He nodded, an amused smile on his lips. But the smile vanished quickly and was replaced with what looked an awful lot like bone-deep sadness. "I wasn't expecting him to say any of that, Mom. He's different now, and I don't understand why."

"I don't either," Joy said quietly as she did everything she could to keep herself under control. Rage coiled in her belly, and she wanted nothing more than to rant about her ex, call him every name in the book, and then eviscerate him for upsetting his son so much that he sideswiped a tree. She rose from her chair and walked over to the couch and sat next to him. "You know I love you... unconditionally, right?"

He smiled at her. "I do. And I'm sorry for being weird about telling you. I knew deep down you would be cool, I just let my nerves get the better of me."

She slipped her arm around his shoulders and gave him a sideways hug. "I love you, K. And I'm sorry your father was such an asshat that it made you nervous to talk to me."

"It's not your fault," he said, leaning into her just as he had when he was a little boy. The contact filled her heart and made her feel whole again.

"You're right. It isn't my fault," she said. "It's his. And I'm going to make sure he knows exactly how I feel about it."

He pulled away and eyed her. "I don't need you to fight my battles for me, Mom."

"I know. But I'm your mom and he's your dad. If it were anyone else, I'd butt out. But on this one, I can't let it go. That's not who we are as parents, and I'm going to remind him of that."

Kyle shook his head but reached for her again, and he hugged her so tight that she could barely breathe. But she didn't care. It was one of those moments she knew she'd remember for the rest of her life.

CHAPTER TEN

*J*oy's head ached and her eyes were gritty when she came awake the next morning. She stretched and peered blearily at the clock on her bedside table. It was after nine, far later than she normally woke for the day. She contemplated getting up and finding breakfast, but instead closed her eyes again and rolled over, intending to grab a few more minutes of sleep.

"Oomph," someone said from the other side of the bed.

Paul, she thought and then wondered why he wasn't at work.

Wait! What the hell was Paul doing in her bed? Joy sat bolt upright and clutched the covers around her as if the man hadn't seen every inch of her in every conceivable fashion. She glanced down at the slender form, intending to kick him out of her bed, her home, and her life, but then she blinked and realized the person wasn't Paul at all.

No, Paul's doppelgänger had somehow found her way into Joy's bed. "Britt?" she said to her twenty-four-year-old daughter. "What are you doing here?"

Britt pushed her short blond hair from her forehead and stared up at her mother with red, sleepy eyes. "Hi," she said simply.

"Hi." Joy smiled down at her. "When did you get here?"

"About three a.m." She sat up and tugged at her old One Direction T-shirt. Britt had been a huge fan of the band as a young teenager and had gotten the shirt at the concert the pair of them had attended. "I tried to wake you up, but you were completely out. You even mumbled something about leaving you alone and not coming back for five years."

"I did?" Joy asked with a laugh. "It's been a rough few days with very little sleep." Joy peered at her, noting the mascara smudged under her eyes along with the dark circles, and concluded she wasn't the only one who'd been missing sleep lately. She reached out and took her daughter's hand. "What's wrong, sweetheart?"

Tears filled Britt's eyes, but she shook her head as she sucked in a shaky breath.

Joy gave her a soft smile. "You don't have to talk about it if you don't want to, but I'm here for whatever you need."

Britt leaned into her mother, resting her head on her shoulder.

They were silent for a long time as Britt cried and Joy rubbed her back and soothed her hair.

When Britt's tears finally dried, she said, "Can I move home?"

"Of course you can, but what about Dave?" Joy's heart ached for her daughter. She'd been with her boyfriend since they were seniors in high school, had stayed together through college, and then had moved to a town thirty miles away where they'd both gotten jobs in their chosen fields of study. Dave was in marketing, and Britt was an accountant like her father. "Is he coming with you?"

She shook her head.

"All right. Kyle's taken his old room. You'll need to take Hunter's since yours has been turned into a home gym," Joy said.

"I see how it is; the boys' rooms remain, but mine was the first to be remodeled. I always knew you couldn't wait to get your hands on my French doors," Britt teased, though her eyes were still sad.

Joy chuckled. Britt's room had beautiful French doors that led out to a deck with the hot tub she'd thought might spark some life back into her and Paul's love life. Too bad that hadn't worked. Paul never wanted to soak in it and in the end, Kyle had ended up using it more often than anyone else. "It does make a good exercise room." She hugged her daughter tighter. "But I'd have given up the equipment and the French doors if it meant you'd have stayed forever."

"Good, because I think this move might be permanent." She let out a choked sob and buried her face in Joy's chest, her entire body shaking as she succumbed to the pain she was feeling.

Joy held on, murmuring soothing words of love and support as her heart broke for her daughter. She didn't have a clue as to why Britt had left Dave, but her baby girl was hurting, and Joy would've done just about anything to bear that pain for her.

Finally, when Britt's sobs quieted, she pulled back and looked around for the tissue box Joy usually left by her bedside. Joy didn't want to tell her she'd used them all up when Paul had left, so she slipped out of the bed and grabbed a fresh box from the linen closet in her bathroom.

"Here." Joy handed the box to her daughter and then wrapped herself in her terrycloth robe. As Britt cleaned herself up, Joy sat on the edge of the bed and waited.

Britt balled the tissues up and stared at the mess in front of her.

Joy knew her girl. She wanted to talk. All Joy had to do was wait her out.

When Britt finally found the courage to speak, she looked Joy in the eye and asked, "Mom, why did you and dad break up?"

Joy stared at her daughter, more than a little surprised. "That was not at all what I thought you were going to say."

Britt gave her a sad smile. "You do realize that none of us know what happened, right?"

"Yeah. I do." There was a good reason for that. Joy herself didn't even really know what had happened. She and Paul had been growing apart, but Joy hadn't thought it was so bad that it couldn't be put back together. Then she'd come home one night to find Paul had packed a bag and said he didn't want to be married anymore. Now her daughter wanted answers, and Joy couldn't blame her. She cleared her throat. "Your dad and I just weren't moving on the same path anymore, I guess."

"That's not a real answer, Mom," Britt said, reaching out and slipping her hand in Joy's.

"I know, honey. The problem is that I don't really know what happened. Your dad just decided he didn't want to be married to me anymore, and he left."

"That's it? That's not a reason," she insisted. Her eyes narrowed and her lips pursed with indignation. "You didn't even ask him to go to counseling?"

Joy couldn't help it. She let out a bark of humorless

laughter. "Oh, honey. Of course I did. I'd been asking him for months to go to counseling. I knew we weren't connecting anymore and wanted to change that. But he didn't. And there's really nothing I can do to change how he feels or force him to stay with me. Besides, I don't want to be married to a man who doesn't want me." Emotionally or physically. But she didn't say that part. There were some things her children didn't need to know.

"He just gave up on our family," Britt said, her indignation turning to outright anger as her face flushed pink. "What the hell is his problem?"

"Britt, he didn't give up on you or your brothers, did he? Doesn't he call you all the time and take you to lunch every couple of weeks?"

She nodded slowly. "Yeah. He took me out last week. But it's not the same as it used to be. He's quiet and never talks about his life. He just asks me about work and Dave and when we're going to tie the knot." She turned a pale shade of green at the mention of marriage, and Joy was convinced she was going to lose the contents of her stomach. But then she rallied. "I guess he isn't a fan of his little girl living in sin."

"Living in sin? What is this, 1958?" Joy chuckled. "Trust me, he doesn't care about that. He's probably just flailing around for something to talk about."

"Really?"

"Really. He wasn't even sure we should get married. I'm convinced he would've been happy to just live together forever if I hadn't insisted."

Britt's eyes widened. "What? I never knew that. So you're saying he never wanted to be married in the first place? Is that why he left?"

Joy took a moment to think about her daughter's question. Then she shrugged. "I don't really think so. But maybe? We were living together and the next thing I knew, I was pregnant with your brother. And then I insisted we get married. We were starting a family, and I wanted it to be legal."

"Why? Doesn't Dad always say that marriage is just a piece of paper?"

"Just a piece of paper." Joy snorted. "That piece of paper made it so that I walked away from this marriage with fifty percent of our marital assets and am not struggling to make ends meet because I haven't been working for the past twenty-six years." She turned, giving her daughter her full attention. "Listen, Britt. I'm a feminist. You know that. Women have choices and should be free to exercise them however they see fit. Kids without marriage is fine. I don't have a problem with it. But when one partner gives up their career potential to raise the children, that partner needs to be protected. Marriage is a legal contract. Remember that."

Britt frowned. "You make it sound like a business transaction."

Joy gave her a smile. "It is, kind of. I have a friend who always used to say that you marry for love, but divorce is a business transaction. I never thought your father and I would get divorced. Not even when we were going through rough patches. I was in it for good. But he decided he needed a different life, and in the end, I'm okay. So is he. We don't hate each other, and we have three children who we love more than anything. Life happens. We just need to deal with it and try to move on."

"I don't know what to do," she said, leaning back against the headboard and closing her eyes.

"About what?" Joy asked.

"Dave." She shook her head. "He got a job offer in Texas and wants me to go with him."

Joy's stomach rolled at the thought of her daughter moving out of state. But she kept her expression and tone neutral. This had to be Britt's choice. "How do you feel about that?"

Her eyes flew open and they flashed with anger. "I'm mad as hell. He didn't even tell me he was applying for that job. It's not even a step up from what he's doing now."

"So why does he want to go?" Joy asked, trying to get to the root of the issue.

She sighed. "It has better growth potential. One of his buddies went to work there and is trying to lure him away. The problem is, he didn't even talk to me about it. He just applied, got the job, and as he was typing up his notice, he asked me to go with him. Like an afterthought."

Warning bells went off in Joy's head, and she wanted to throttle Dave. She liked him well enough, but that wasn't how a partnership worked. "Does your opinion count at all in his decision to move?"

"No. Not at all. He's going with or without me. He says it's the opportunity of a lifetime and he wants me with him, but he can't pass it up." Her shoulders slumped. "He didn't even take into consideration that I just got a promotion at work or the fact that I make thirty percent more than he does right now. If I leave this job and try to find something in Texas, my income will take a hit and I'll have to leave a job I really love."

"I'm sorry, Britt. It sounds like he didn't take you into consideration at all." Joy didn't want to bad-mouth her daughter's partner, but she for damned sure wasn't going to sit there and let her daughter think what he'd done was acceptable. Sure, he'd asked her to go with him, but he'd made decisions about their life together without considering her needs or consulting her first.

"That's what I said, and then we had a big fight about it. He told me I wasn't being supportive. I told him he was being selfish. And it went downhill from there. Then I left to come here because I was too upset to sleep." She sighed. "I don't know what to do."

Joy wanted to tell her to leave his selfish ass and find someone who treated her better, but even she knew that there were two sides of the story, and Joy would always take her daughter's side, no matter what had gone down. "I can't answer that for you, Britt. Only you know what's most important."

She squeezed her eyes shut and shook her head. "That's not helping, Mom."

Joy chuckled. "I know. Adulting sucks."

Britt sucked in a deep breath and opened her eyes to peer at Joy. "Would you do it all over again?"

"Do what? Marry your dad?"

"Yes. If you knew then what you know now, including Dad leaving you and you sacrificing a career, would you have done it anyway?"

"Yes," Joy said without hesitation. "Absolutely no question. If I didn't, I wouldn't have three kids I love more than life itself. But even so, I liked our life. Your dad and I loved each other and had a true partnership for a lot of years. The fact that we've parted ways doesn't change that. It just means we have a new path from here."

Britt narrowed her eyes. "Why do I get the feeling you're sanitizing this for me?"

Joy held her hands up and chuckled softly. "I might be toning down my disappointment in how things turned out, but

I absolutely do not regret any part of it. I loved being home to raise you kids and working at the Arts Market. Now I'm off on another adventure. That's all life is, you know. An adventure. You just need to decide if Dave is going to be part of yours."

"I could stay here like Aunt Hope," she said.

"You could. That was the right choice for her, and in the end, she still got her Prince Charming."

"But she had to wait for thirty years for him," Britt said with a snort of irritation.

"True. But if you asked her the same question you just asked me, I bet she'd say she doesn't regret her decision. She's led a life full of love, and if she and Lucas had stayed together way back then, they probably would've stifled each other and ended up apart anyway. They both needed to walk their individual paths before they were ready for what they have now."

"This isn't helping," she said with an air of frustration. "You're my mom. You're supposed to tell me what I should do."

Joy reached over and pulled her daughter into a hug and whispered, "Welcome to adulthood."

"You're evil." Britt climbed out of bed and started to pull her clothes on.

"Maybe. But it's still a question only you can answer. Which is more important? Your job and staying here close to home? Or Dave and a new adventure?"

"Ugh." She turned to stare out the window. "Why couldn't he have talked to me about it first? Maybe then I wouldn't have been so blindsided."

Joy moved to her daughter's side and placed a hand on her back. "It sounds like you two need to talk. Make sure you understand where he's coming from and that he understands your concerns. Then the two of you can decide."

Britt turned to her. "That sounds suspiciously like the adult thing to do."

"You are twenty-four."

"I hate you," Britt said, but she was smiling when she draped her arm over Joy's shoulder and added, "Let's go make breakfast. I'm suddenly hungry."

CHAPTER ELEVEN

"*K*ye Kye!" Britt called as she ran into the kitchen and wrapped her arms around Kyle, who was sitting at the table with a mug in front of him.

"Kye Kye?" Jackson said, both of his eyebrows raised. "Since when are you a thirteen-year-old girl?"

"Shut up," Kyle said, shaking his head at Jackson while leaning into Britt's hug.

Joy stood in the doorway of the kitchen just watching them. Britt and Kyle had been really close when they were young, but then the teenage years happened, and Joy had often wondered who was going to kill the other first. But now? They were two peas in a pod when they got together.

"Hey, Jackson," Britt said as she gave him a quick hug from behind. "Long time no see. What have you been up to? Or should I say, *who* have you been up to?"

Kyle let out a choked cough, while Jackson stared at him, clearly wondering what he should tell Britt.

Joy cleared her throat. "Have you boys eaten?"

"Just coffee," Kyle said.

"Do you want breakfast?" she asked, heading for the refrigerator.

"Sure. Thanks, Mom."

"Jackson?" she asked, glancing over her shoulder.

He stood up and shook his head. "No thanks, Joy. I need to get home and change for work."

"What? You're leaving?" Britt asked. "But I haven't seen you in ages."

"Sorry, B. You know how it is when you gotta work for the man." He smiled at her and turned to go.

"Wait," Kyle said, catching his hand and stopping him.

Jackson stared down at their clasped hands and then looked him in the eye. "Wait for what?"

"This." Kyle tugged him close and then pulled him down for a quick kiss. "See you tonight?"

Jackson grinned at him. "I'll come over after work." He quickly glanced at Britt, who was staring wide-eyed with her mouth open. He gave her a wave as he chuckled and then all but floated out of the room.

"Well done, Kyle," Joy said with a wink.

He flushed bright red, but a smile made his lips twitch.

"Kyle!" Britt cried. "You're the guy Jackson is doing?"

"Britt!" Joy barked. "Please. His mother is in the room."

Kyle's face turned a deeper shade of red. "I, uh, wouldn't put it like that. But yes, we're dating."

"And he stayed the night!" She flopped down into the chair across from him. "Scandalous," she said, pressing her palm to her chest.

Kyle rolled his eyes. "I have a broken leg. How scandalous could it have been?"

She pursed her lips and gave him a cheeky smile. "I'm willing to bet it wasn't PG13." Britt turned to her mother. "You're allowing this, Mom? I mean, they're just teenagers."

Joy snorted while Kyle groaned.

"You do remember that I'm twenty-two years old and a college graduate, right?" he asked her.

"You'll always be my sweet sixteen-year-old brother. I just can't deal with your boyfriend sleeping over." She reached over and ruffled his hair.

"Oh for the love of the gods," he mumbled. "I'm not inviting you to the bachelor party."

"Bachelor party? You're engaged?" she cried as she stood so fast the chair nearly fell over. "Just what exactly has been going on all these years? How long have you been together? And why didn't you tell me?"

Joy stood at the stove, frying bacon and chuckling to herself as Kyle launched into an elaborate story about how they'd been star-crossed lovers ever since high school. Joy knew the truth of course. He'd admitted last night that they'd only been together about a month. He'd dated one other guy in college, but it hadn't been serious enough to talk about.

"I hate you," Britt said without any heat. She continued to ask him questions and express her unwavering support.

Joy reveled in the fact that two of her children were home. Her heart swelled with love and contentment at the sound of family at her table. She'd missed them. And while she was enjoying her freedom to start a career and prioritize her interests for the first time in years, there was nothing better than being with her children, two of the three people she loved most in the world. She knew they needed to grow up and make their own lives without their mother hovering in the background, but there was a small part of her that desperately wanted them to move home and stay there forever. She just enjoyed them. And as far as she was concerned, there wasn't a damn thing wrong with that.

"Hey, Mom?" Britt called.

"Yeah?" Joy turned around to look at her children.

"Do you want to tell us why you have purple dots all over your face?"

Joy frowned. "What?"

Britt pressed her forefinger to her chin, her forehead, and then two spots on her right cheek. "You look like you got into a fight with a purple Sharpie and lost."

Dread curled in Joy's gut as she hurried down the hall into the bathroom. When she looked at herself in the mirror, she let out a loud groan. Sam's facial had finally seemed to work on the acne, as the bumps had vanished, but the dark purple spots had been left in their place. "Britt?" she called. "How long are you staying?"

Her daughter appeared in the doorway. "I'm not sure yet. Why?"

"I'm going to need your help tonight." She pointed to her face. "I have a cocktail party to go to… with press. And I cannot look like one of the Purple People Eaters."

Britt, who'd always had an interest in makeup, laughed. "All right. Don't worry about a thing. I've got this."

* * *

"I THINK YOU NEED A REAL HEALER," Britt said as she dabbed yet another layer of concealer on Joy's face. "These marks only seem to be getting darker."

"I know. Pretty soon I'm going to look like I have flesh

eating bacteria on my face." Joy had to admit that she was really getting concerned. She'd started to wonder if someone had cursed her or if the remedies she'd tried had caused the unusual spots. "I just need to get through tonight, and then I'll go see Carrie at Luminal Space Day spa. She'll know what to do."

"Are you sure you don't want to try this stuff Gigi gave you?" Britt looked at the small jar and bit her bottom lip.

Joy sat back in her chair and sighed. "I tried it last night. It didn't seem to do anything."

"Crap. All right. I'll get these spots covered, but it's going to be a lot more makeup than you're used to. And no snuggling up next to your date. You'll get makeup all over him."

"Fine. Just as long as the pictures are good, that's all that matters."

"I'm on it."

An hour later, Joy's spots were hidden under a pound of makeup, her hair was styled into a fashionable twist, and she was wearing a dress that hugged every one of her minimal curves. She walked out into the living room with a thigh-high boot Hope had insisted she buy in one hand and a stiletto in the other. She held them up for her children. "Which one?"

"The boots," they both said in unison. Britt turned to Kyle. "You're on your way to becoming a really fabulous gay man."

"I'm not gay. I'm bi, and that was a terrible stereotype. You should be ashamed of yourself," he said before turning back to Joy. "Mom, you look hot."

Joy grinned at him. "Thanks, Kyle. I feel a little overdone, but—"

"Not overdone, Mom," Britt said. "Like Kye Kye said, you're gorgeous. Movie star material. Troy had better appreciate you, because if he doesn't, the rest of the world is going to be lined up to take his spot after they see you in that dress."

Joy smoothed her black and silver cocktail dress and smiled gratefully at her daughter. "I have to admit that this was not what I expected to be wearing at forty-eight years old."

"Yeah, we had you pegged for muumuus and obnoxiously bright leggings with oversized shirts that hide your butt," Britt said with a wide smile. "But then you had to go and turn into a fancy model and actress, and now we have no choice but to watch you strut around here like Heidi Klum. I tell you; it's exhausting just keeping up."

Joy chuckled and retreated to her room to get into her boots. She was just touching up her red lipstick when she heard the doorbell ring. Her hands started to shake so bad, it was a miracle she didn't end up with red lipstick all over her face.

"Calm down, Joy. It's just Troy. Relax," she told herself in the mirror.

"So, Troy," she heard Kyle say from the living room. "I hear you're dating our mother. Does that mean you've been keeping it in your pants while you've been out of town, or have you been—"

"Kyle!" Joy cried as she rushed down the hall and into the living room. "Stop interrogating the man."

Troy let out a long low whistle. "Joy Lansing? Is that you?"

She grinned at the tall man with the kind blue eyes and felt a rush of heat run down her spine. Damn, he was handsome. The memory of running her hands through his thick dark hair swam in her memories, and she was certain that, given a chance, she'd gladly do it again. "It's me. In the flesh."

He walked over and leaned in, giving her a gentle kiss on her cheek. Then he whispered, "You are smokin' hot."

"Thank you. You're not so bad yourself. I'm sorry we didn't get a chance to talk much at your gallery show this afternoon. The place was packed, and I didn't want to bother you."

"You're never bothering me, but thanks for coming out. It made my day."

Kyle cleared his throat, and Joy looked over to find him with his arms crossed over his chest, eyeing Troy suspiciously.

"What is it, Kyle?" she asked, giving him a look that told him to behave himself.

"I just wanted to know what time we can expect you home tonight."

Troy glanced between Kyle and Joy and then chuckled. "Do you have a curfew, Joy?"

"I don't know. Do I?" she asked Kyle, giving him a warning tone.

"Of course she doesn't," Britt cut in. "We just wanted to know if you're coming home tonight. We don't want to worry."

Kyle let out a grunt but didn't say anything else.

Joy shook her head. "Just this morning I was thinking how nice it was to have you guys home. Now I'm wondering how much longer I'm going to have to put up with you two freeloaders."

Britt snorted while Kyle rolled his eyes. He looked at Troy and said, "Don't let her fool you. I'm fairly certain that if I gave her the greenlight, she'd go over to my apartment and pack everything up herself if I told her I wanted to move home permanently."

Troy grinned at her. "You know, after spending a little time with her, I'd have to say you're probably right." He walked over to the couch where Kyle was elevating his broken leg and held out his hand. "It's nice to meet you, Kyle. I'm Troy."

Kyle reluctantly shook his hand but still nodded an acknowledgement.

Troy turned his attention to Britt and charmed her immediately with a kind smile and by complimenting her shoes.

Joy laughed and tugged him out of the house. On her way out, she called over her shoulder, "I'll be home tonight sometime. Don't wait up."

They both called after them, Kyle protesting and demanding a time and Britt reminding them to not forget protection.

"They're colorful," Troy said as he opened the passenger door of his Toyota Sequoia.

"They're a pain in my ass," she said, stepping up into the SUV.

He leaned in and said, "You like it though."

Chuckling, she nodded. "I do. They're fun."

He shut the door, and in no time, he was in the driver's seat, steering the vehicle down the road toward Prissy's cocktail party.

"Your photos from Europe are really spectacular," Joy said. "I especially liked the ones in that small town in Italy that documented everyday life. The emotions you managed to capture were breathtaking. I mean, the range… you really have a gift, Troy."

He flashed her a wide smile. "Thanks. But really, it's the people who allowed me to photograph them that deserve the credit. They were just being themselves, and I somehow managed to capture a small piece of them."

"That's humble," she said kindly. "But we both know it takes a special eye to capture that kind of emotion. I think my favorite is the older couple who were sitting on a bench, holding hands with their heads bent together while smiling at each other. I made up an entire story in my head about them being married for fifty years and still being deeply in love even after weathering countless obstacles."

"You're actually not that far off," he said, looking amused. "They've been married for forty-eight years, have nine children, buried two, and have reinvented themselves three different times to stay afloat. And they still really like each other. There's a ton of love there. I just hope I did them justice."

"You did," she said simply.

He glanced over at her, his cheeks flushed slightly. Then he cleared his throat and asked, "So, what did I miss in Premonition Pointe?"

Joy stared at his handsome profile and shook her head. "What didn't you miss? You've been gone for... I don't know how long." She shrugged. "Everyone thinks we're dating, thanks to that interview you did. Filming has come to a halt because Prissy threw a temper tantrum. My son broke his leg in a car crash. And well... you know about Carly's niece."

Troy glanced at her. "That's a lot."

"Yeah, but I'm handling it," she said with a shrug.

"Of course you are. Since we're headed to Prissy's cocktail party, why don't you tell me why she threw a tantrum?"

Joy let out a sardonic chuckle. "I called her a hateful bitch on set."

He snorted. "I bet she deserved it."

"She did." Joy studied him, noting his amused smile. "Do you know her?"

"Nope. But when she kept trying to get in touch with me about her cocktail party, I asked a couple of people who are in the position to know her. None of them were terribly impressed with her personality."

"So why did you agree to go with me?" Joy asked curiously.

"Because you asked me to," he said simply.

"That's… really kind."

"I had an ulterior motive," he admitted.

"Oh, yeah? Do tell."

His eyes glinted in the evening light. "It turns out that the person who asked is the same person I'd been dying to see this weekend. The same one I'd like to be dating, if she's open to it."

"Dating? For real?" she asked.

"Sure. You're single. I'm single. We already know we enjoy each other. Why not?" He flipped his blinker on and took a right turn into a gated community.

She thinned her lips and tilted her head as she considered him. "Can I ask you something?"

"Sure. Shoot."

"Did you date anyone while you were in Europe?"

"Date?" he asked, his eyebrows raised.

Joy huffed. "Okay, fine. Did you sleep with any of your models?"

He stiffened as he cocked one eyebrow at her. "Is that what you think of me?"

She wasn't sure if that was righteous indignation or a redirect. "It's what happened with us. We'd known each other less than a day before we fell into your bed. I guess I just wondered if that's a normal thing for you."

When he didn't answer, she started to fidget and added, "I just want to know what I'm getting into. That's all. I… shit." She turned and glanced out the window at the large beach houses on Seaside Lane.

"You what?" he prompted.

"This isn't what I want to be talking about right before a cocktail party hosted by Prissy, but I guess since we've already landed on this, I'll just spit it out. You're the only person I've been with since my husband and I separated. I don't usually do casual, although, obviously I was all for it in the moment. I'm not trying to be judgy; I just know myself. And if you're seeing other people then—"

"I'm not seeing other people," Troy said. "And I didn't fall into bed with anyone while I was gone. I had no desire to. Every night when I went to bed, all I could see was this gorgeous blonde who's so sexy, and all I could think about was getting back here and finding a way to get *her* back into my bed."

Joy's face flushed, and she couldn't help the grin that claimed her lips. "Um, that was lovely."

He winked at her. "Now, as to those dating rumors in the press, why don't we confirm them tonight? And if we survive this cocktail party, I'd love to take you somewhere a little less hostile. Say my place tomorrow night? I'll cook."

"Your place, huh?" she asked, grinning.

"Yes. I haven't eaten a home cooked meal in forever. If I have to go to one more fancy restaurant, I might start to bleed butter. My place. I'm an excellent cook."

"Now that's an offer I can't refuse," she said just as they pulled up to a circular drive in front of the largest house on the street.

"It's official then?" he asked.

"Official."

"Good. Are you ready for the freak show?" he asked, nodding to the crush of paparazzi outside of the SUV.

Prissy must've called every gossip rag on the planet, because Joy had never seen so many photographers in one place before. She took a deep breath and said, "I guess I'm as ready as I'm ever going to be."

"Famous last words," he said with a chuckle. Then he opened his door and was met with an onslaught of flashes from the cameras. Before she even knew what was happening, Troy was there, opening her door and tugging her down a red carpet where all of Prissy's guests were posing for the cameras.

CHAPTER TWELVE

The flash of the cameras blinded Joy as Troy led her down the literal red carpet that bordered a hedge of Prissy's rental. She remembered Prissy warning her about the paparazzi but hadn't expected that she'd actually set the house up as if it was some sort of premiere. Talk about pretentious. How desperate must she be to invite that sort of over-the-top attention?

"You're going to want to start looking like you're happy to be here," Troy whispered in her ear.

She blinked up at him. "I don't look happy?"

He chuckled. "You look like the only reason you want to go inside is to stab someone. Likely Prissy."

Joy couldn't help but laugh. "You're not wrong about that one."

"Joy! Joy! Over here!" one of the photographers called.

"Can you comment on your relationship?" another one asked.

"How's filming going? We heard rumors there was trouble on the set."

On and on, the strangers demanded answers to invasive questions. Meanwhile, Troy kept his hand on the small of her back, reminding her to smile for them and to not react to anything they said.

"Is it true your son is gay?"

She immediately stiffened and scanned the photographers, looking for whoever was asking about Kyle.

"Ignore them," Troy insisted as he tugged her into him and then smiled cheekily at the cameras before bending her backward and kissing her full on the lips.

Joy's immediate instinct was to push him off, but before she did anything that would cause even more of a stir, his words sank in. *Do not react to anything they say.*

Shit! They'd found a weakness, and she was one hundred percent sure that Troy's over-the-top antics were to distract the press so no one would notice how she'd reacted to the question about her son.

"Thank you," she whispered when he finally righted her again.

"My pleasure." He winked at her and then waved to the camera as he guided her into the large modern home that overlooked the sea.

Joy was grateful for Troy's quick thinking, but she couldn't stop wondering how the press knew about Kyle. Or why they'd been looking into her kids in the first place. The bone-deep feeling of violation made her nauseated. She couldn't imagine one of her kids being highlighted in a gossip rag just because she was working on a movie. They didn't deserve that.

"Hey," she asked Troy once they were inside, "is there anything I can do to stop them from writing about my kid?"

He frowned, glanced around the room, and then led her over to a quiet corner. "I doubt it. If they print outright lies, you can sue and try to force a retraction, but the problem there is that the more you say or fight, the bigger the story is. If you want to keep them out of the limelight, the best thing to do is just never talk about them and dodge questions when the press asks."

"That's what I have been doing, but one of them was asking questions about Kyle. He's not a part of this." She waved a hand wildly, indicating the house, the photographers, the industry she'd chosen. "I just wanted to act, not have my family dragged through the tabloids."

He gave her a sympathetic smile. "It's all part of fame, though. And once the genie is out of the bottle, there's no stuffing him back in. There's no telling how the press will behave or how interested fans are going to be. The only thing we do know is that if there's money to be made by selling a story, there isn't much you can do."

She groaned. "I don't want this for them. Especially Kyle. He doesn't deserve to have his love life speculated about in the papers."

"Is he out? Publicly, I mean?"

"What?" she asked, startled. But she recovered quickly. "No. I mean, I don't think so. He just told me and his sister this weekend that he's dating Jackson. I don't even know if his friends know, though I'd assume they do. One of his best friends is a lesbian. I can't imagine why he'd keep it from her. And there's really no reason to hide." She shut her mouth, realizing that she was rambling. "Sorry. I'm just thrown, that's all."

He wrapped his arm around her shoulders and pulled her in close to him. "No need to apologize. Your son's privacy is being threatened. I'd be pissed too."

Joy wrapped her arms around him, hugging him. And even

though she was still worried about what the press might do, she felt a little better just being in his arms. "Thanks. Who knew that even being a D-list celebrity was going to be so stressful?"

He chuckled. "Babe, you are the furthest thing from D-list."

"Troy Bixby!" Prissy called, appearing suddenly in the foyer She was wearing a strapless, floor-length dress that had a slit up to her hip on the left side. She gave him a huge grin and made a beeline for him without even acknowledging Joy's presence. "I have been dying to see you again."

"You two have met?" Joy asked. Hadn't Troy told her on the way over that he didn't know Prissy?

"Not that I know of." He held his hand out to Prissy and said, "Hello. It's nice to meet... see you again. Please, refresh my memory. How do we know each other?"

"Oh my gosh, silly. I'm sure you remember me. We met at that gallery opening in LA last year. We made plans to get drinks at Chill."

Troy frowned. "Chill?"

It was obvious to Joy that he wasn't acting. He genuinely had no idea what she was talking about.

"That hot new rooftop bar in Hollywood? We were going to meet there, but then your brother called because his car broke down, so we agreed on a rain check." She slipped her arm through his and held on. "I guess tonight is that rain check."

Panic flashed in Troy's eyes as he glanced at Joy. "Uh, yeah, that all sounds vaguely familiar. But tonight I'm Joy's date, and I—"

"Joy can take care of herself. Can't you, Joy?" Prissy gave her a cat-that-ate-the-canary grin. "Besides, it's good for her career if she works the room."

"I don't—" he started.

"Troy Bixby!" A very familiar tall man with jet-black hair called out, cutting him off as he rushed over and gave Troy a bear hug. When he let him go, he grabbed his arm and patted him on the shoulder. "How long has it been, brother?"

"Zack Hayes! How long *has* it been, man?" Troy grinned at him. "I don't think I've seen you since graduation day when you crashed your motorcycle into that bouncy house. Man, Greek row was pissed at you. They were planning to hold wet T-shirt contests in that thing."

Joy snickered. It sounded exactly like what might have happened at her college.

"Oh, Zack," Troy said, nudging Prissy out of the way. "This is my girlfriend, Joy Lansing. Joy, this is Zack Hayes. We went to college together."

Joy held her hand out to him and nearly died when she realized he wasn't just Zack Hayes, college friend, he was Zack Hayes, television star of the popular family drama *Summer Creek*.

"It's a pleasure to meet you, Joy," Zack said, shaking her hand.

"You, too," she croaked.

Prissy rolled her eyes. "Oh. My. God. Please don't tell me you're starstruck. I'm so embarrassed for you." She turned to Zack. "My apologies. The director of my new film took a liking to Troy's photos of her, and now I'm stuck mentoring a newbie on set. I'm sure you know how it is, Zack."

The actor stared down at her and then shook his head. "You're a piece of work, aren't you, Prissy?"

She shrugged. "I'm just voicing my truth. Don't tell me you don't get tired of being fawned over. I know you too well, Zack. This party is supposed to be a place no one has to worry about that." Prissy shot Joy a look of disgust. Then her eyes narrowed, and she leaned into Joy and tapped her chin as she whispered, "Tell your makeup artist she missed a spot."

That familiar rage that filled Joy's gut every time she had to deal with Prissy reemerged, and Joy had to fight to not sneer at the younger woman. Or claw her eyes out. But Joy was the mature one, and fighting with her costar would only cause more problems. She pasted a smile on her face and said, "You're so helpful, Prissy. Thank you. I'll let her know."

Zack peered at Joy. "What the hell are you talking about, Prissy? If you ask me, Joy's the most beautiful woman here."

"As if," Prissy mumbled and grabbed both men by the arm. "You two are with me. There's someone you both need to meet."

"I'm going to pass. Like I said, I'm Joy's date," Troy said, trying to shrug her off. But she held on tight.

"Oh, no. You're not getting away this time, Troy Bixby. You owe me a drink. Joy will still be here after we've taken care of business."

He opened his mouth to protest again, but Joy shook her head, knowing that if Prissy didn't get her way, filming on Monday would be filled with her never-ending tantrums. The entire reason she'd brought Troy there in the first place was to appease the actress. "You go ahead, Troy. It's fine. Besides, Prissy's right. There are some people here I need to say hello to."

"Are you sure?" he asked, a faint note of pleading in his tone.

Her lips twitched, and she gave him a half smile. "It's okay. I'm sure."

It took a little work, but he did manage to escape from Prissy's death grip long enough to give Joy a searing kiss. By the time he let her go, she was slightly winded and her lips tingled. "Wow."

He winked at her and then turned to Prissy. "All right. Let's get this dog and pony show on the road."

Prissy glared at Joy but then put on a bright smile and said, "Troy, do you like blow jobs?"

"What?" he asked and stared over her shoulder at Joy. He mouthed, *Help!*

"The drink. They're called blow jobs. They're the theme of the party. No one ever says no to a blow job."

Joy rolled her eyes and mouthed back, *Good luck.*

"I'm down for a blow job," Zack said. "Great idea, Prissy."

Joy shook her head, and instead of working the crowd as Prissy suggested, she made her way to the open bar for a glass of wine and then stepped out onto the balcony and settled into a chair to listen to the waves.

CHAPTER THIRTEEN

*J*oy wasn't sure how long she'd sat on the lounge chair, but she'd have been content to stay there all night. Making small talk at a cocktail party with a bunch of self-important industry people was the last thing she wanted to do. But daydreaming about living in a beach house and having an evening cocktail on the balcony every night kept her quite entertained.

Unfortunately, Prissy found her, ruining Joy's good time. She dropped into the deck chair beside Joy and let out a disgusted snort. "What *are* you doing, Joy?"

"Relaxing?" she asked, not quite sure that's what she'd call it.

"You're flushing your career down the toilet; that's what you're doing." She held out a martini glass that was filled with pink liquid. "Here. Drink this. It will at least make you look a little less like a loser."

Joy sat up and took the drink. But instead of thanking her, she said, "What do you want, Prissy?"

"What makes you think I want anything?" she asked. Her

brows were pinched, and her lips curled in disgust. "Maybe I just don't want anyone at my party looking like she's so uncool that she has to sit by herself drowning in her sorrows."

"I'm not drowning in anything, Prissy," Joy said with a sigh. "I actually enjoy listening to the waves crashing below. And since you insisted we show up and then immediately stole my date, I'm doing what I enjoy until you release him." She smiled sweetly at Prissy. "You get what you want, and I get what I want. It's a win-win."

"You're pathetic." Prissy said as she rose from the chair. "Enjoy your drink. And don't expect your date back until after midnight. I have plans for him." Prissy smirked and floated off back into the house.

Joy stared after Prissy and felt all of her Zen from the ocean slip away. The woman was pure spite. What she didn't understand was why. Joy hadn't done anything to her. And she certainly wasn't a threat. Prissy was a young, gorgeous, sought-after actress. Joy was a forty-eight-year-old mother of three who was just starting out in the business. Was it about Troy?

Joy glanced through the windows and spotted Prissy hanging all over him. Troy, to his credit, looked like he was ready to chew his own arm off just to get away from her. It was time to rescue him. She downed the sweet pink drink Prissy had brought her and then made her move.

Or at least she *tried* to make her move. Just as she was headed back inside through the open sliding glass door, she was jostled to the side and let out a cry as she lost her footing and started to go down. Two strong hands grabbed her just before she wiped out and pulled her upright, setting her back on her feet.

"Whoa, there. Are you all right?" the man asked.

"Yeah. Thanks for that. Wiping out would've been a little more humiliation than I could handle tonight."

He chuckled and said, "Happy to help, ma'am."

His deep baritone was a delight, and she grinned at him. "Of course, it was your fault I almost broke an ankle, but since you saved me, I'm willing to overlook it."

"Thanks." He jerked his head toward the open bar. "Can I buy you a drink?"

She glanced over where Troy had been and frowned when she realized he was no longer there. Neither were Prissy or Zack. "Did you see where Prissy went?" she asked her new acquaintance.

He waved a hand toward the other end of the house. "She dragged her harem after a photographer. Pretty sure she's blackmailing someone into publishing pictures of her hanging all over them."

"Harem." Joy let out a humorless laugh. "She stole my date."

"Stole? More like he's a jackass for leaving your side for hers. That woman is a lot to deal with."

This time when Joy laughed, it was real. "I appreciate the sentiment, but he's only humoring her for me. I have to work with her, and she's kind of making my life hell."

"So… that means you must be Joy Lansing, right?"

"Uh, yeah." She gave him a questioning glance. "How did you know that?"

"I read." His lips curled into a sexy half smile.

Joy rolled her eyes. "Seriously? You've been reading the gossip rags?"

He laughed. "No. Not usually. Actually, I was booked for a part in your movie. So I'll be on set on Monday." He held out his hand. "Quinn Redmond. Nice to meet you."

"Quinn?" She shook his hand. "Seriously? You're the guy

who plays my younger… um, love interest?" She squeezed her eyes shut and shook her head. "Why do I feel so awkward about this?"

Still holding her hand, he pulled her closer and whispered in her ear, "It's the sex scene."

She groaned, and they both laughed. "Yeah. That's gonna be terrifying."

"Not for me," he teased. "Hot woman, people watching… what's not to like?"

If anyone else had said those words to her, she probably wouldn't have laughed. But his sarcastic tone made it all too clear he was going to be just as nervous as she was. "We'll get through it, right?"

"Just as long as Prissy isn't watching. That woman is so cold, I bet she could suck the heat out of the sun if she could manage to get close to it," he said with a mock shudder.

"You know what, Quinn?"

"What's that, Joy?" he asked.

"We're going to be good friends. And I'm thrilled you've joined the cast." She slipped her arm through his exactly the way Prissy had done with Troy and Zack earlier and glanced up at him. "How do you feel about spending the rest of this booze fest out on the balcony?"

"You're not coming on to me, are you, Joy Lansing?" he asked, raising his eyebrows in suspicion.

"You wish." She mock-punched him in the arm. "I'm just trying to survive this cocktail party without dealing with any pukers or tweakers. You're not either of those things, are you?"

"Nope. Lead on." He waved a hand at the balcony.

She let out a sigh of relief and hurried back outside just as a group of five twentysomething actresses were headed straight for them, each of them double fisting their drinks.

"Quinn!" one of them called. "I've been looking for you. I need a lap to sit on."

"Go!" he urged, and the two of them pushed their way through the crowd and then hightailed it out of the party and back onto the deserted balcony.

"Oh, thank god," Quinn said when they turned to look back at the party raging inside. The pack of women who'd been headed straight for him had been sidelined by a group of guys on the prowl. They either weren't too discerning, or they were too drunk to care. Considering one of them was pounding the contents of three solo cups, Joy was guessing they were too drunk.

"So, if you're Joy, that means you're dating Troy Bixby, huh?" Quinn asked as they leaned against the railing.

She glanced over at him. "Something wrong with that?"

"No." He held his hands up in a surrender motion. "His photos are pretty outstanding. I was just wondering how you two met. From what I hear, he doesn't really do industry parties anymore."

"We met here in town. He has a house here." She frowned at him. "What do you mean he doesn't do industry parties anymore?"

He shrugged. "His ex used to drag him to all the hottest parties, but at some point, he just stopped going. In fact, I think he avoids most publicity other than his gallery openings and prearranged interviews to promote his work. The rumor is he had a run-in with the paparazzi that didn't go well."

But Troy had come to Prissy's event without question because she'd needed him to. Her heart sped up, and she wanted nothing more than to go back in the house and pry him from Prissy's grasp and take him home. Or out for pie. The man was a saint. She was about to get up and do just that, when Quinn placed a hand on her arm. She looked down and then back up at him.

"Have you heard from Carly?" he asked.

Joy studied him. "Do you know her?"

He nodded, his expression solemn. "We were in a show together last year on Broadway. *Mama Mia.* She was really fantastic. I know her neice, too. Ever since Harlow went missing, I've been thinking about them." He dug into his pocket and pulled out his phone. After searching a bit, he passed it to her.

Joy gazed down at the photo of Quinn with one arm around Carly and the other around Harlow. All three of them were smiling as if they'd just been laughing. She could practically feel the affection radiating from them. She glanced back up. "I've seen her. She's doing about how you'd expect. Hanging in there, stoic, but really worried."

"I'm sick about Harlow. She's…" He glanced away and swallowed hard. "Anyway. They need to find her."

He looked so sad, so lost that she reached out and squeezed his hand. And in that moment, her world spun. When it righted again, she was back in the bedroom where Harlow was being held. Only this time, Harlow wasn't the only person in the room.

A short man with spikey blond hair was hovering over her, demanding to know when Carly was going to pay the ransom.

She turned to look up at him with defiant eyes, but didn't say a word. Joy wanted to cheer. The woman had a fire in her and wasn't giving up despite her incarceration.

"Get her to pay up, or the boss will show up," the blond man wearing faded jeans and a black T-shirt snarled. "And trust me, once he's here, all bets are off."

The scene faded, and Joy found herself back on the balcony

of Prissy's beach house, still clutching Quinn's phone and breathing hard.

"Joy, are you all right?" he asked.

"Yeah. I'm all right. I just…" She glanced around, frantically looking for a pen and something to draw on. She grabbed a cocktail napkin that was lying on a small table next to the deck chairs and asked, "Do you have a pen?"

He patted his pockets and shook his head. "No. Why?"

"I need a pen. Right now." She handed him his phone and hurried back into the house, heading straight for the bar. But before she got there, she ran into Troy.

He grabbed her hand, stopping her and staring down at her with a worried expression. "What's wrong, Joy? What happened?"

"I need a pen. Right now. It's important."

Without a word, he reached into his suit pocket and produced a silver pen.

"Thank you," she breathed and perched on the edge of a nearby chair as she quickly sketched the guy she'd seen in her vision. When she was done, she said, "We need to go."

"You got it." He grabbed her hand again, and without either of them saying their goodbyes, they walked out of the party and rushed to Troy's car, this time ignoring the cameras and onslaught of questions.

Once they were in his SUV, he sped down the street and asked, "Where to?"

"Carly's. I have information she needs."

He glanced over at her, his brows furrowed. "You realize it's past eleven, right?"

"I do. This can't wait."

Troy nodded and said, "Point me where I need to go."

CHAPTER FOURTEEN

"*H*ere. The one here on the right," Joy said, pointing to Carly's beach rental.

Troy pulled to a stop against the curb and glanced around. "I would've thought there'd be at least a few paparazzi considering everything that's going on."

Joy scanned the area and let out a sigh of relief. She'd anticipated being mobbed again, and had been worried about how they'd spin that story in the gossip rags, but Harlow was more important than worrying about bullshit stories. "I guess they're all at Prissy's for the evening. It's not that surprising, I suppose. Carly hasn't been giving them much to print since she's been holed up in her house and not going anywhere."

They hurried up to the front of the house, and just as Joy was about to knock, the door swung open, revealing Baldy, the guard who'd given her and Hope a hard time the day before.

"What are you doing here?" he barked. "Do you know what time it is?"

Joy took in his bare feet, faded blue jeans, and the long-sleeved shirt that had obviously been hastily buttoned, causing the buttons to be misaligned. "Yes, I do. I need to speak to Carly. It's important."

"Come back tomorrow." He started to slam the door, but Troy put his hand out, stopping him.

"Ms. Lansing said it's important," Troy said, his tone full of steel. "We aren't leaving until she talks to Carly."

"Oh, no?" The guard reached around to his back and pulled out a Taser. "I guess we'll just see about that. You two are trespassing, and if you don't get out of here right now, I'll see to it that you regret that decision."

Joy narrowed her eyes at the man, ready to claw his eyes out. "It's about her niece. Remember what happened the last time I was here and you tried to keep me from Carly?"

"You seem to be under the impression that Ms. Preston was cross with me for initially stopping you from seeing her," he said. "But you'd be wrong. It's my job to protect her from people who don't have her best interest at heart. And from where I'm standing, Ms. Lansing, that's usually most people. So forgive me if I don't make it easier for you to invade her privacy."

"Look, Baldy," she started.

"Gary," Carly said from behind him, cutting Joy off. "It's all right. Let Joy and her young man in."

He turned to look at her and shook his head. "We do not know who he is, and it's far too late in the evening for anyone to be calling. Whatever this is about, it can wait until I can run some checks on them."

Carly patted him on the arm patiently and said, "There's no need for that. I trust them." She waved to Joy. "Come in. Bring Troy with you."

Joy smiled triumphantly at Baldy as she brushed past him. But as soon as she was in the house, her smile vanished.

There was no space to be petty about a man who was obviously just trying to do his job, even if Joy thought he was being a jackass about it. She'd had a taste of what the press could take from a person, and she was already questioning if she'd made the right decision by pursuing acting. Considering Carly was a world-famous actress who'd dealt with unwanted intrusions for years, she must've felt like she lived her life in a fishbowl.

Carly was wearing a white silk robe over matching white silk pajamas, and despite her face being free of makeup and her hair tied up into a messy bun, the woman was still flawless. Her skin glowed, and if it hadn't been for the worry lines around her eyes, Joy could've easily mistaken her for a woman much younger than she actually was.

"Take a seat," Carly said, waving to the armchairs opposite her white couch.

Joy did as she was told, but Troy stood behind her, his hand resting on her shoulder in an unspoken gesture of support. She glanced up at him, giving him a grateful nod. Joy glanced over at Baldy, who was standing in the entrance to the living room with his arms crossed over his chest. Joy met Carly's eyes. "I had another vision." Then she glanced at Baldy. "Do you want me to…" She waved a hand at him. "Should he hear this?"

"Why wouldn't he?" Carly asked, bewildered.

Because he's the one who wanted to sell a story to the press? Joy thought to herself, but trying to be tactful, she said, "Um, you might want to keep what I have to say private."

Carly glanced at him and then back at Joy. Her expression turned to one of comprehension as she seemed to understand what Joy was implying. "Oh. Right. Um, that issue we talked about before, it's all taken care of. Gary here is trustworthy."

Baldy, er Gary, gave Joy a smug look. "I don't sell stories to the press. Whatever your friend thought she heard, she was wrong."

Joy shuffled her feet back and forth, feeling very uneasy. Baldy hadn't given Joy any reason to trust him. He'd been rude, crude, and downright disrespectful. Why had Carly let him in her house? A horrifying thought occurred to her. What if Baldy was blackmailing her or using information about Harlow to manipulate her? Did she need to get Carly out of there?

"Carly," Joy said. "Can I just talk to you in private for one moment?"

Carly once again glanced at Baldy and then back at Joy. "Anything you say to me, I'm just going to tell Gary anyway. It's really fine, Joy. I promise."

Joy didn't like it. She didn't like it at all, but really, what choice did she have? "You're sure?" she tried one more time.

Carly nodded, giving her a reassuring smile. "I'm sure. Now what did you need to tell me?"

"I had another vision." She held the napkin with her drawing on it out to Carly. "This is the person who has her."

Carly let out a gasp and pressed her hand to her chest as she stared at the napkin. When she looked up, she asked, "Was he hurting her?"

Joy shook her head. "No, not physically anyway. He was standing over her, shouting about a ransom. It appears he did this for money."

The actress leaned back on the couch and let out a weary sigh. "I was afraid of that." She glanced at Baldy. "Did you know about this? The ransom?"

Baldy gritted his teeth and flexed his fingers.

"Gary?" she asked, her tone demanding now. "Don't lie to me. I'm already angry enough that you left me in the dark."

"Fine. Yes, I know." He stared back at her, his expression hard. "It's an obscene amount of money. And if you cave and pay it, you'll solve one problem but invite a hundred more. Once people realize you'll pay anything to keep your family out of harm's way, they'll be gunning for everyone you care about within a week. You cannot pay this ransom. I forbid it."

"Oh, you do, do you?" Carly challenged. "Who do you think saved you from getting your ass thrown in jail this week?"

"I didn't do anything!" he shouted.

"No, but you were planning to." She stood and looked down at Joy. "Can I keep this?"

"Yes," Joy said. "But then I won't be able to take it to Detective Coolidge."

"I'm on it. I'll call her in the morning." Carly walked over, kissed Joy on the cheek, and said, "Thank you. I need to make a phone call now."

To the private investigator, Joy assumed. Once Carly left the room, Joy focused on Baldy.

"Who are you to her? And why were you going to be thrown in jail?"

"That's none of your concern," he said with a sniff. "Now, it appears your business is done here. I'll show you out." He waved his hand, indicating she and Troy should shuffle their way toward the door.

Joy didn't move from her spot on the couch. "Listen, Gary," she said, hoping by using his name, he'd start to behave a little more human. "You haven't exactly impressed me as a standup guy. You make a show of protecting Carly, but how do I know you aren't just trying to take advantage of her?"

"Take advantage of her? You mean, like, for her money?" he asked, scratching his neck.

"Or... other things," she said, trying to get a read on him to see if he was being as inappropriate with Carly as he had been with Hope.

"What other things?" he asked, looking genuinely confused.

"You know, *other things,*" Joy stressed, but when she said, 'other things,' her voice squeaked and she had trouble getting the words out.

Both of the men just looked at her while she swallowed. Was that a tickle at the back of her throat? When Gary didn't respond, Troy covered his mouth and faked a cough as he said, "Sex."

Gary blinked at them. Then, as he realized what Troy had said, his face scrunched up into a look of disgust and his entire body shuddered. "You think I'm trying to get into Carly's pants?"

Joy shrugged.

"Oh, god. No. Just no." He covered his ears with his hands and started shaking his head. "That image in my head is going to put me in an early grave."

"All right! That's enough," Joy demanded. This time her voice was definitely scratchy. Man, that was the last thing she needed. She ignored her rapidly deteriorating voice and continued, "It's clear you're not into Carly. No one can act that well. Not even Carly."

He shuddered again. "It's not an act."

"Obviously." Joy winced at the knives now attacking her throat and stood, determined to continue her verbal assault on the man. "Okay, then tell me why you seem so hell-bent on not helping her. Or at the very least, why you're trying to keep me away from her." She swallowed hard and forced herself to continue, despite the pain she was feeling. "I'm only trying to help."

"Yeah, well, so am I. And if history is any indicator, Carly can't trust strangers. And you're a stranger. All I'm doing is protecting my... client." He finished his statement as if he'd been going to say something else. Friend? Girlfriend? Money train? Joy didn't know, but it looked like she wasn't going to get a chance to find out because Gary had already moved to the front door and had it open. "Goodnight Ms. Lansing. Goodnight Mr. Bixby."

"Tell Carly to call me anytime if she needs me," Joy said.

"I'll relay the message," he said dryly. "Now go before you infect either of us with your germs."

She glared at him but let Troy guide her out of the house.

Once they were outside and back in his SUV, Troy asked, "Are you okay?"

She grimaced as she shook her head. "No. I don't know where this frog voice came from, but I'm in serious need of an herbal treatment."

"Do you have a supply of herbs at home?" he asked.

She nodded, swallowed, and winced once more from the pain as she leaned her head against the window.

Troy reached over and grabbed her hand. "Just relax. Once we get you home, I'll make you my mom's secret sore throat miracle cure."

She raised an eyebrow at him. "She taught you herbal remedies?"

"Yep. She taught me everything I know in the kitchen. She was an earth witch, so she had a lot of tips. The time I spent with her as a teenager is why I love to cook." He squeezed Joy's fingers.

Joy suddenly remembered he was supposed to make her dinner the next night, but the chance of that was looking grim if she had strep throat. She prayed she didn't, because she really wanted to see that man in an apron.

CHAPTER FIFTEEN

The sound of the phone ringing jolted Joy out of the best dream she'd had in months. She'd been watching Troy move comfortably around her kitchen, and he'd been completely naked, save her *Kiss the Cook* apron. And man, was he gorgeous. She especially liked watching his muscular butt as he stood at the stove steeping the herbs for her throat. She'd been about to sneak up on him and finally grab onto his glorious globes when the damn phone had woken her up.

The ringing stopped before Joy managed to grab it from her nightstand. She rolled over and groaned when she saw it wasn't even eight o'clock yet. Who the hell was calling that early on a Sunday morning?

The phone started chiming again, and she grabbed it, finding Paul's name lit up on the screen. Unease settled in her gut. Something was wrong. He'd never call that early otherwise.

Hunter.

Her breath caught as she thought of her oldest son. Was it

him? Their other two children were safe in Joy's home. She quickly answered. "Paul?" she croaked. Her voice was barely audible, but at least the stabbing pain had vanished. She cleared her throat and tried again. "Paul?" The word came out clearer even though her voice was still husky. "What's wrong?"

"What's wrong?" he thundered on the other end of the line. "What's wrong? What isn't wrong?"

Joy climbed out of bed and grabbed a pair of jeans out of her closet. Irritation formed in her chest, and she couldn't help snapping back, "I don't know, Paul. Why don't you tell me instead of biting my head off?"

"You did this to our family, Joy. Didn't you ever even stop to think what it would mean for me and the kids when you decided to start running around with those Hollywood types?"

"Did what?" She grabbed her toothbrush and filled the brush with toothpaste. "I have no idea what you're talking about."

"Read the *Premonition Perspective*. You have ten minutes before I get there." The call ended abruptly, and Joy stared at the phone with her lip curled in disgust.

"Who the hell do you think you are?" she asked the phone as she tossed it down on the bathroom counter. She took a moment to settle down, and then stared at herself in the mirror. She looked tired and like she could use a facial, but at least the purple spots had faded and were almost gone. It was the one bright spot of her rude awakening. After going through her morning routine, she emerged from her bedroom in jeans and a T-shirt and headed straight for the coffee pot.

"You're up early," Britt said from where she sat at the table. She was wearing leggings and a long sweatshirt, with one foot on the seat of the chair and the other on the floor.

"Not that early," Joy said. "It's not like I sleep half the day away every day."

"Did you smoke a pack of cigarettes last night or something? You sound like Mrs. Barker," Britt said, referring to the ninety-four-year-old woman who sold incense and friendship bracelets at the Arts Market.

Joy shook her head. "I started to come down with something last night, but Troy made some miracle herbal tea that knocked it out. Now I just sound like death."

"Not death," Britt said, pulling a knit cap over her short hair. The cool breeze from the nearby ocean was wafting through the open window. "More like a phone sex worker."

Snickering, Joy poured a cup of the coffee that Britt had already made and grabbed a donut from a bakery box on the table. "Did you get these?"

She shook her head. "Lex dropped them off last night when she came by to see Kyle."

"That was sweet of her." Joy took a long sip of her coffee and then a large bite of the glazed donut. It wasn't long before the sugar and caffeine combination worked their magic and Joy finally felt human. She glanced over at her daughter. "All right. How bad is it?"

"How bad is what?" Britt asked in a tone conveying innocence.

"You're not fooling me. Your dad already called to yell at me. I know something made the papers."

She sighed, lifted her right butt cheek, and pulled the paper out from underneath her. As she passed it over, she scrunched up her face and said, "It's pretty bad. Mostly for Kyle."

"Kyle?" The coffee curdled in her gut. They'd written about her son. The bastards!

Britt frowned. "There's a few unflattering pictures of you, too."

Joy waved a hand, unconcerned about that. All she really cared about was protecting her kids. She put down her coffee and donut, opened the gossip rag, and cringed when she saw the picture. She was climbing into Troy's SUV, and the photo captured her with her legs open, giving everyone a clear shot of her black underwear. To top it off, her mouth was open and she looked as if she were yelling at someone. The effect made it appear she was running from the paparazzi and pulling a diva moment with the press. "That's attractive," she said dryly.

"Sorry, Mom." Britt pushed the donut closer. "You might want to choke that down before you read the article."

"I doubt it. I'm already on the verge of losing what little I have in my stomach." She turned her attention to the headline.

Joy Lansing, freshly divorced, freshly dating, and running from questions about her troubled gay son.

Joy let out a gasp. "What the hell?"

"I told you it was bad." Britt grabbed another donut and shoved it in her mouth.

The article was full of made up lies and pure trash.

Joy Lansing spent the last thirty years in a troubled marriage. Within six months of her husband leaving her, she posed for racy photos, landed a supporting role in an upcoming film under suspicious circumstances, and abandoned her injured son after he came out as gay. To say that Joy Lansing is a problematic woman would be an understatement.

"Problematic? This is the most sexist, misogynistic, homophobic piece of trash I've ever read. How can they make up such lies?" she cried, glancing around widely as if she had an audience bigger than her daughter.

Britt climbed out of her chair and rushed to her mother,

wrapping her arms around her in a tight bear hug. "It's one hundred percent lies, Mom," she said. "Anyone who knows you won't believe a word of that. You know that, right?"

"Yeah, but this is going to kill any hopes I have for a career if stories like this keep circulating. Who's going to want to cast a forty-eight-year-old drama queen?"

Britt opened her mouth to say something, but stopped when the front door crashed open and Paul called, "Joy!"

"Oh, shit," Joy muttered and buried her face in her hands.

Britt reached over and rubbed her mom's arm soothingly. "Don't worry. He'll get over it."

Paul barged into the kitchen, holding a copy of the *Premonition Perspective* up in the air. "What the hell were you thinking going to a drug-fueled Hollywood party half naked?"

"Dad!" Britt yelled, turning to face him. "You're out of line."

The tall man with thick black hair and plastic black-rimmed glasses did a double take when he saw his daughter standing in Joy's kitchen. "Britt. Why are you here so early?"

She placed her hands on her hips and glared at him. "I'm home for the weekend, visiting my mother. If you hadn't just up and left her, I'd be visiting you, too."

"Britt!" he admonished, scowling at her. "That was unnecessary."

"Was it?" she shot back. "How dare you come in here and yell at Mom while you're off starting a new life without us!"

He took a step back and then blinked at her. "That's not—"

Britt held a hand up to stop him. "No. I don't want to talk about this right now. I have other important life matters to deal with." She spun around and met her mother's gaze. "I'm going to go check on Kyle."

Joy nodded and stared at her ex until Britt disappeared down the hall.

"Britt's never spoken to me like that before," Paul said, his tone cold. He crossed his arms over his chest and stared Joy down. "See what kind of example you're setting for your daughter?"

"The kind of example *I'm* setting?" Joy asked incredulously. He'd lost his damned mind. "You have some nerve."

"Me?" he scoffed. "I'm not the one going out and acting like a fool in some pathetic attempt to reclaim my youth."

The amount of rage building in Joy's blood was almost more than she could handle. Her entire body started to vibrate, and she had to mentally talk herself down from decking him. She sucked in a deep, cleansing breath and in the most neutral voice she could muster, she said, "You have no idea what I'm doing. And you gave up the right to know when you decided you didn't want to be married to me anymore. So save your lectures for someone else. I'm not going to stand for it."

"The whole world knows what you're doing!" he roared as he brandished the paper at her. "When you run around like a twenty-year-old whore, don't think I'm not going to step in when our kids are involved."

"Whore?" She threw her head back and laughed. "That's rich. Since when did you become a misogynist?"

"I'd imagine that was right about the time he became a homophobe," Kyle said from behind his father. He was dressed, his hair tamed, and leaning on his crutches.

Paul's shoulders hunched at the sound of his son's voice. He turned around and looked at him warily. "Kyle. I didn't realize you were here."

"Why would you? You haven't even called to check on me since my accident. I figured you didn't give a shit. If you did, you'd probably have stopped by or texted or hell, even asked Mom how things were going. But instead, I suppose you're too uncomfortable with the fact that I'm dating a guy. So who cares that I broke my leg, right, Dad?"

"I'm not a homophobe," Paul insisted. "I'm not."

Joy snorted. "Is that why you told him to find someone with a better job and preferably a woman so he could start a family?"

Paul sank down into one of the kitchen chairs and ran a hand through his hair. His face was pale and gaunt, and Joy thought she'd never seen him look older. "I don't have any hard feelings toward Jackson," he said to Kyle. "I just don't think he's your intellectual equal. It's going to be hard enough to be in a same-sex relationship. You don't need the added problems of dating someone who doesn't have your drive."

Joy met Kyle's gaze, and the hurt she saw reflected there made her want to eviscerate her ex. Her heart was breaking for her son, but as much as she wanted to fillet Paul, she recognized that she needed to let Kyle fight this battle. Still, she was his mother, and she couldn't stop herself from saying, "Whatever your opinion is on his relationship with Jackson, it probably would've been nice if you'd at least inquired as to how his leg is, Paul. He did break it after all."

"Shit," Paul muttered and turned back to his son. "How is your leg?"

Kyle rolled his eyes. "It's healing. Mom, Britt, and especially Jackson have been taking care of me."

Paul nodded. "That's good."

"It is good," Kyle said, his tone quiet. All of the anger seemed to have drained out of him, and Joy thought he just sounded sad. "You know what else is good, Dad?"

"What's that?"

"My relationship with Jackson. He's my best friend and a really great guy. He's also ambitious and is so much more than a guy who just works at the coffee bar. Not that this matters, but he's also opened his own graphic design business. He's smart and kind and just about the best person I know. So if you plan on having a relationship with me, you won't ever imply that he isn't good enough for me again. Got it?"

Joy's heart swelled with pride. Her little boy had grown up to be a brave young man who wasn't afraid to speak his mind.

"I didn't mean to imply that," Paul insisted.

"Yes, you did. And while I'm at it, I decided against law school and am going to be a writer. One way or another, that's what I'm going to do. If it doesn't work out, I'll find something else. But don't try to tell me my chosen profession isn't good enough. It will only drive a bigger wedge between us." Kyle stared at his dad for a long moment. When his dad didn't respond, Kyle sought out his mother and caught her gaze.

I love you," Joy mouthed to her son.

He gave her a faint smile. *Same.*

Paul stood. "I guess I deserved that."

"You're damned right you did," Joy said, unable to hold back any longer. "And if you even think about devaluing our child again or implying there is something wrong with who he chooses to love, our next conversation is going to be a lot more volatile. Understand?"

Paul ignored Joy and walked up to his son with his arms open. "Can I get a hug?"

Kyle frowned slightly but then nodded. "Yeah."

Finally the man Joy had married appeared, and he gave his son a long hug with a pat on the back. When he pulled away, he said, "I'm sorry for my reaction. It was clearly out of line, and I'm proud of how you've handled yourself today."

"All right," Kyle said, clearly still upset about his father's behavior but obviously trying to make peace. "Thank you for that. But if I'm being honest, I have to tell you that the way you've been treating Mom this morning is even worse than the way you treated me when I came to see you. She doesn't deserve your wrath. All she's done is take a part in a movie and start dating a pretty nice guy. If you can't handle it, that's your problem. She deserves to be happy."

"That's not exactly all she's done," Paul said, waving the gossip rag again. "She's embarrassed the family and brought hateful comments into your life. She needs—"

"The only thing she needs to do is finish making that film. Anything else, including dating Troy, is up to her," Kyle shot back. "And as far as bringing hateful comments into my life, do you really think I'm so naïve that I didn't realize some people would have shit to say when they found out I'm dating a man? Come on, Dad. Give me more credit than that."

Paul stood there with his mouth hanging open.

Joy shook her head at him and then moved to give her son a hug of her own. Once she had him in a tight embrace, she whispered, "I'm really proud of you."

"You, too, Mom. Don't let him berate you. I saw the article, and it's complete shit. Ignore it." He kissed her cheek and then gently pushed her back. "I've said everything I need to say. I'm going to rest my leg. Try not to kill each other, all right?"

Joy waved as Kyle nodded to her and then crutched his way down the hall.

Paul turned back around and stared at Joy. "When did he get to be so grown up?"

She lowered herself into one of the chairs and sighed. "He's been grown up, Paul. You just haven't been paying attention."

Her ex clutched the back of one of the chairs and stared at the floor. Finally, when he looked back up, he said, "You're right. Can we go out back? I think there are things to say."

141

Joy wanted nothing more than to throw his ass out after the way he'd behaved when he'd barged in their house, but there was a hint of desperation in his expression and after all their years together, she found she just couldn't say no. She stood, grabbed her coffee and her uneaten donut, and said, "Follow me."

CHAPTER SIXTEEN

*J*oy curled up on the swing and watched as Paul milled around the backyard as if he were inspecting the landscaper's work. She sipped her lukewarm coffee and just waited. There wasn't much she wanted to say to him other than to tell him to get out and never come back. But she knew that was just her temper talking. She'd loved the man for many years. If he wanted to have a mature conversation, she could do that... as long as he behaved.

Paul stood at the firepit and without looking at her, he said, "I had to leave."

"That seems fairly obvious."

He ran a hand through his hair again, making the black locks stick up in wild, untamed clumps. "No, Joy. I *had* to go." He turned and stared her right in the eye. "I wasn't giving you what you needed, and it was killing me. I've spent the last five or ten years trying to figure out why I couldn't be the person you needed me to be."

Joy clutched her mug tighter and ground her teeth

together. "If this is another lecture about why it's my fault you left, you can save it, all right? I don't need to hear this again. I've got it, okay? I was too demanding, and you couldn't take the pressure. Whatever. You're free. You left and I didn't stop you. That's the end of it. Just don't continue to ignore your children or butt into my life, and we'll be just fine. Got it?" She got up and started moving back into the house.

"Joy! Wait." He reached out and grabbed her wrist, stopping her from bailing on their conversation. "That's not what I meant. Can you please…" He sighed. Just let me try to get this out before you hand me my ass again, okay?"

"Uh, well, when you put it like that, I guess so." She took her seat in the swing, crossed her legs and waited.

Paul started pacing again, paused, and then sat across from her in one of the deck chairs. "Roughly about ten years ago, I realized that I didn't have much of a sex drive."

Joy raised her eyebrows, surprised this was what he wanted to talk about. Though maybe she shouldn't have been. Their sex life, or rather lack of one, had been one of their major issues. They'd never had a robust sex life, but when the kids had been young, Joy hadn't had much energy and hadn't really thought much of it. But as they grew older and Joy hit her late thirties, she'd wanted and tried desperately to rekindle their time in the bedroom. Nothing had really worked. But she'd never considered leaving him. Though she had tried over and over to try new things or get him to go to counseling. Paul had always been resistant. "Okay. I always assumed you were using porn to take care of your needs. Why didn't you say anything?"

He let out a huff of humorless laughter. "How do you tell your wife, whom you love, that you don't want her sexually?"

A stab of pain shot her right in the heart, and she knew it

must've shown on her face, because he grimaced and let out a groan.

"I'm sorry, Joy. It really had nothing to do with you and everything to do with me."

She shrugged. "All right. So, why tell me now?"

"Because you deserve to know the truth."

Joy glanced away, trying to collect her thoughts. Then, without looking at him, she asked the question she'd asked when he'd told her he was leaving. "Was there someone else?"

"I already told you there wasn't," he said.

It was true. He'd denied ever having an affair, but she hadn't really believed him. Now though, as she peered at him, she could tell that he was being completely honest. "Okay. And that's why you left? Because you didn't want to have sex?"

"Yes. No. Maybe both?" He sat back in the chair and stared up at the blue skies. "I went to a therapist."

"What?" She leaned forward, shocked by his admission. "You said you didn't want to do that."

"I said I didn't want couples' counseling. I was terrified to tell you how I was feeling. Joy, imagine having to sit down and tell your partner you aren't attracted to them when you desperately want to be. I tried everything. I watched every kind of porn to try to get into the mood. Remember when you found the link to the anal plugs?"

Joy's cheeks heated as she remembered ordering some for them to try, and when they showed up, they were intercepted by his mother. The only saving grace was that she hadn't known what they were. Even so, it had been mortifying. "Yeah. That's not something I'm likely to forget."

"I was watching that and trying to determine if maybe that would help things. Or decide if I was really into men. Or... I don't know. The truth is, I'm just not into *any* of it. And worse, I don't want to be anymore."

"So you're saying you left this family because you're what… asexual?" she asked.

He moved and sat next to her on the swing and took her hand in his. "Yes, that's what I realized at therapy. Finally. I had a lot to work through for myself and my image of what a man should be. And here you are, a gorgeous woman who deserves to be worshiped. I just… I couldn't pretend anymore. I needed to live my truth."

Joy couldn't help but feel hurt. She just felt gutted by his admission. It wasn't that he wasn't attracted to her. She knew enough to understand that sexuality was on a spectrum and could change over time. No, she was upset because he'd felt like he couldn't talk to her. That he had to leave their life together in order to feel whole. "Um, I don't know what to say."

"You don't have to say anything. I just thought it was time you knew the truth. None of this was about you. It was all about me. And in the end, I realized that I was making us both miserable."

"And to fix it you felt you had to leave." She knew they were just talking in circles now, but she was still processing. It wasn't easy to hear that the man she'd loved and intended to spend the rest of her life with just didn't want her, even if logically she understood she wasn't at fault.

"I did." He dropped her hand and scooted over, putting more space between them.

"I'm sorry," she said automatically. "I'm just… This is hard for me to hear. I understand, though, and appreciate you telling me."

He nodded.

They sat in silence for a while, both lost in their own thoughts until Joy blurted, "This conversation isn't why you came by today."

"Nope. Not even close." Paul rubbed his eyes and let out a long breath. "I was wrong to come tearing over here like that."

"So why did you, exactly?" she asked curiously. "That's not usually like you."

He hung his head. "I saw all that crap in the paper and just lost my mind. The thought of having our family business out there for everyone to see and comment on terrified me, and I took it out on you."

"You realize none of that is true, right?" she said testily. "It's made-up garbage to sell gossip rags."

"Yeah. I do now." He turned to eye her. "I'm sorry. I'm actually really proud of you for chasing your dream. When it comes down to it, that's part of the reason I decided it was time for us to go our separate ways. I wanted you to have the freedom to live your life, to blossom into the person I always knew you were supposed to be."

What a load of crap, Joy thought to herself. She wasn't buying any of his rationalizations about why he left. It was clear to her that he needed to get out for him. Whatever his issues were, his sexuality or realization that he needed to live a different life, he did it for him. Maybe he thought he was being noble and giving her the space she needed for a new life, but he'd hurt her deeply by shutting her out so completely the last years of their lives together. If he'd really left for her, she absolutely deserved to have had a say in it. But he hadn't given her the option. And now it was done.

The thing was, she just didn't want to talk about it anymore. If he needed to frame it as if he'd done something good for her to make himself feel better, she was willing to let him have that. She'd come to terms with her life without him. It was time for them both to just move on.

"So, what are you doing for a social life these days?"

A slow smile claimed his lips, and a tiny spark lit his gaze. "Lots of golf, a weekly poker game, and I've taken up fly fishing out in the river. It turns out I love spending hours out there."

"That makes sense." He'd always been one to enjoy his solitude. She patted his knee and rose from the swing. "I'm glad. You seem more at peace."

"I am."

He got to his feet and followed her back into the house.

Joy led him to the front door and patted his chest. "Thank you for being honest. That explains a lot."

"I guess it would."

She gave him a small smile. "You and I are good, Paul. Just remember that your children have their own issues to work out, and yelling at them about their life choices isn't going to help them get past this. Try to be patient and understanding, okay?"

He pursed his lips and narrowed his eyes at her. "It would help if you had my back."

This time she didn't bother to hide her eyeroll. "Paul, if you had any idea how many times I've stood up for you, you'd be kissing my feet. I've told them repeatedly that whatever happened between us didn't have anything to do with them and that you still love them. Now it's up to you to take it from here. Got it?"

"Um, yeah. Got it." He gave her one of his big hugs, apologized, and then left.

Joy watched until he drove off and then quietly shut the door on their past.

CHAPTER SEVENTEEN

*L*ife was funny sometimes. Joy had spent her morning listening to her ex have a temper tantrum over bullshit that he should've seen through right away. And then that same night she found herself in a gorgeous beach house, tucked in the corner of an incredibly comfortable leather couch, while a very sexy man handed her a dirty martini. A fire crackled in the fireplace, setting the mood for an epic romance.

"Thank you." Joy smiled at Troy, thankful that her voice had returned. It had been scratchy most of the day, but after Gigi called to check on her, she'd heard the problem and delivered a tonic that had cleared it right up. She took a sip of the martini and said, "It's perfect. Did you tend bar in college or something?"

"Actually it was after college." His face lit up with the memory. "It was a small town Back East, and that's how I paid my rent while I did my apprenticeship with a world-renowned photographer. He was a complete ass, so it was nice to have a place to go blow off steam even if I was the one behind the bar."

"And you said your mother taught you to cook, right?" Troy had been true to his word. He was an extremely good cook and had made them salmon risotto. It was by far the best risotto she'd ever had, and she might have moaned her way through the meal.

Troy nodded and took a sip of his beer. "My mom was a chef. She had her own restaurant, and I used to help her out on weekends."

"You are a man of many talents." Joy ran her gaze over him and didn't miss the spark of heat that flashed in his eyes.

"Right back at ya, Joy Lansing. Model, actress, psychic, and fantastic mother. Tell me, is there anything you can't do?"

"Well, as it turns out, I'm not great at outrunning the paparazzi. Those bastards managed to take the most unflattering picture of me on the planet. I also flashed the world my underpants, so there's that." She raised her glass to him in a mock toast. But when he didn't touch his glass to hers, she frowned. "Is there something wrong?"

"What? No." He shook his head. "Of course not." He eyed her and added, "That picture wasn't that bad. At least your legs looked good."

She rolled her eyes and threw a pillow at him. "So you saw the article?"

His good humor vanished, and his eyes flashed with a hint of darkness. "I saw it. It was everything that is wrong with the entertainment industry. I'm sorry, Joy. You and your son didn't deserve that."

"No, we didn't," she agreed. "But Kyle's fine. I guess there are advantages to growing up in the social media age. He's really good at blocking stuff out and just going on with his life. Me, on the other hand... I was ready to go down to that office and tear some heads off."

"I hear you." He reached out and slipped his fingers through hers. "You didn't do that, though, did you?"

"Of course not. That would just feed the story." She shrugged one shoulder. "It's not like the *Premonition Perspective* is a national gossip magazine. I'm hoping that if we all continue to ignore them that their lies won't spread when the movie comes out."

He grimaced.

"I see you think that's naïve," she said.

Troy tipped his beer to his lips and sucked down half the contents before he answered. "Maybe. But that's only because I've been on the receiving end of some really nasty stories. I did what you are doing right now. I ignored them, hoping they'd go away. But they never did. Or at least not until I disappeared for a while."

"I heard you were allergic to industry parties and photographers."

He let out a laugh. "Yeah. You can say that again."

Joy tilted her head to the side to study him. "If that's true, then why did you agree to go to Prissy's party with me?"

His expression softened, and he squeezed her fingers. "Because you needed the help. And I figured it couldn't be too bad, considering we're in Premonition Pointe instead of Hollywood." He chuckled. "I guess that was a bad bet."

"I'm sorry." She downed the rest of her martini and set the glass on a side table. "I really do appreciate it, even if I'm starting to accept that no matter what I do, there's no way Prissy is ever going to stop her games."

"She does seem too diabolical to be redeemable." Troy winked at her. "Does that mean you didn't enjoy it? Not even when you met Zack Hayes?"

"Goddess no! I hate cocktail parties. Especially when I'm surrounded by a bunch of self-important people. While you were being schmoozed by Prissy, I spent most of my time out on the balcony hiding out."

"You did?" He laughed again. "That sounds exactly like where I would've liked to have been. Instead, I got to listen to Prissy talk about her time in the Caribbean and how she couldn't wait to show me all her favorite spots. I was starting to feel like she might be planning to abduct me by the end of the night and hide me out on someone else's private yacht."

"Someone else's?"

"Yep." Troy brushed his dark hair out of his eyes. "Prissy blows through all of her own money on fancy beach houses and red-carpet parties. Trips and things like yachts are always courtesy of someone else. In that world, it's all about perception. As long as you look rich, you're in the club. The minute you say you can't afford something you're taken out with the trash."

The sudden bitterness in his tone took her by surprise, and she couldn't help prodding, "You sound like you speak from experience."

He put his beer down and leaned in closer to her, bringing his hand up to cup her cheek. "I had a life in LA before I moved here. I'm sure you know that."

"I assumed you did," she said, staring into his intense gaze. "But I don't know anything about it."

He blinked, and then a wide grin took over his face. "You didn't google me?"

She chuckled. "I might have googled a little. But that was to stalk you while you were in Europe. You know, so I could picture which city you were in and get a read on when you might be back here."

Wonder filled his blue eyes, and Joy was desperate to kiss him, but she didn't want to derail their conversation. Now that he'd brought up his past, she was dying to know the details.

"You could've just called me," he said, brushing his thumb over her bottom lip.

Joy closed her eyes for a moment, soaking in his tender touch. When she opened them, she said, "Yes, but then I'd forfeit my chance of playing hard to get."

"I have news for you, Joy Lansing. There hasn't been a moment since we met that I've considered you hard to get."

"Oh, really?" She shook her head in amusement. "Are you saying I'm easy?"

"No. I'm saying that the chemistry between us has been off the charts, and neither one of us has been able to resist the other."

"Damn, that was a good save," she said and then gently kissed the thumb still caressing her lip.

"I thought so." He pulled back and dropped his hand, much to her disappointment. But when he started talking, it was worth it. "Back when I first started making a name for myself in LA, I dated a model. It was important to her to be seen everywhere and on the arm of all the most eligible bachelors in town. She said it helped her book jobs."

"Did it?" Joy asked. She was so new to the industry that she didn't know if exposure like that really helped or if it was all just a giant ego stroke.

"Maybe? Who really knows? She was getting a bunch of

covers and was being asked to walk in fashion shows. Her career wasn't hurting. But because she was 'dating' every actor in sight, the stories about our relationship just kept coming. They made up everything from threesomes to domestic abuse."

"Holy hell, Troy. That's awful," Joy said, horrified for him.

He nodded. "I had galleries lined up all over the country. Everything was going really well, and if you didn't count the avalanche of stories coming out about us, even our relationship was pretty good. Or at least I thought it was."

"It wasn't?" she guessed.

"Nope. Not even close. She actually was cheating on me, and when that came out, all the stories had a hint of the truth and the reporters smelled blood in the water. It became too much. I ended up canceling a bunch of shows and moving up here to get away from it all."

Joy wanted to bitch-slap the model who'd cheated on him and taken advantage of his good nature. How could someone do that to him? This time Joy leaned into him and pressed her hand against his cheek, enjoying the scruff of his five o'clock shadow against her palm. "She didn't deserve you."

"That was the conclusion I came to as well... eventually." He leaned into her touch, his eyes still blazing into hers.

"And after all of that, you still went to Prissy's party and endured all the bullshit you'd left behind," she said, wondering how she'd gotten so lucky to meet him that day at Gigi's party.

"It was you," he said simply. "And I can say without a doubt that you're worth it."

"Damn you, Troy Bixby. That was exactly the right thing to say."

His eyes held hers, blazing with heat, and never before had Joy been so drawn to a man. Her lips parted, and before she even realized what she was doing, she cupped both of his cheeks and kissed him with everything she had.

A low moan slipped from his lips as he kissed her back, their tongues tasting, exploring, and devouring each other until eventually, Troy stood, picked her up, and carried her to his bedroom.

CHAPTER EIGHTEEN

*M*onday morning was brutal. After several emotion-filled days, consistently late nights, and the ongoing turmoil of the visions of Harlow she'd been experiencing, all Joy had wanted to do when she woke up in Troy's bed was roll over and go back to sleep.

Or she did until Troy wrapped her in his arms and made love to her again.

Joy grinned to herself as she thought of the sweet way Troy had made her breakfast and sent her off with a thermos of coffee. She couldn't remember a better morning in all of her forty-eight years.

Unfortunately, once she'd gotten on set, her day had gone downhill rather quickly. She'd walked into her trailer to find that the place looked like a pack of raccoons had invaded and left her with a pile of garbage that smelled so bad she'd run back out, gagging. It was a miracle she hadn't hurled right then and there.

Now she was forced to share a trailer with Prissy, who was having a fit about sharing her sacred space.

"It's just until the crew can clean it up, air it out, and figure out how the rodents got in," the PA said, trying to calm her down.

"I don't understand how that garbage bag got there," Joy said for the fifth time. "I rarely eat in there, and when I do, it isn't fast food or frozen pizzas." The garbage looked like it belonged to a frat boy who gobbled calories for sport.

"There's no need to be embarrassed about your food choices, Joy," Prissy said with a sniff. There was a towel wrapped around her wet hair, and she was wearing a silk robe that barely covered her assets. If she moved just the right way, Joy was going to know if she preferred a Brazilian or a bikini wax. "Honestly, it explains a lot about your complexion. But it is a miracle you don't weigh more. Tell me, do you have a problem with purging? Because if you do, I know someone you can talk to."

"I don't purge," Joy said through clenched teeth. "And that wasn't my garbage."

"Oh, sweetie," Prissy said, patting her arm. "You're just embarrassing yourself now."

Joy turned to the PA. "I'll be in the makeup tent if you need me for anything."

"All right. Check in with wardrobe, too. There's been a change in plan for the scene you're shooting this morning."

Joy was in too big a hurry to worry about what had changed. She just needed to get away from Prissy, the most condescending, immature person Joy had ever met. After checking in with Sam at the makeup tent, who was pleased to see that her skin had cleared up, she headed next door to the wardrobe tent.

"Hey," she said to Vince, the movie's stylist. The short

brunette was wearing skinny jeans and a vest with a bowtie and looked as adorable as ever. "I heard you needed me."

"Oh, thank goodness." Vince hurried over to a rack and pulled out a hanger with two scraps of leather hanging from the hook. "I need you to try this on."

Joy took the hanger and stared open-mouthed at what she assumed was a leather bra and G-string. Only it was hard to tell since mostly they were just strips of leather. "You're not serious."

"Oh, I am," he said, nodding. "There's been a change with the sex scene. Finn wants your character to explore a fetish for the first time with the love interest. The new script is over there on the table." He took the hanger from her and then started holding the triangles of fabric up against her breasts.

"That's barely going to cover my nipples," Joy said, grimacing at him. "Don't you have a sexy corset and thigh-high boots around here or something?" There was a note of panic in her tone that even she noticed.

"Not one for a dominatrix. There's a white lace one and a sexy red number, but Prissy has already worn them. We can't have it looking like you borrowed your daughter's clothes to seduce a younger man. That's just a step too far."

"Seduce?" Joy squeaked out. "I thought he was the one doing the seducing?" Joy's character was strong and confident, but when it came to getting naked with the love interest, her character was supposed to be hesitant due to past experiences. Joy could not imagine a scenario where her character would be wearing leather and acting like a dominatrix. She hurried over to the table and grabbed the script. After scanning the scene, she let out a groan. "This is going to be a disaster."

"It'll be funny, Joy. Come on. It's not that big of a deal," Vince said, pulling out a pair of lacy thigh-high stockings. He gave her a kind smile. "You'll stuff yourself into this outfit and blunder around the stage for a while, and then it will be over. No acting needed."

"You've got that right." Joy had been willing to try many things to get her husband interested in her over the past several years, but leather and whips hadn't been one of them. Mainly because Paul would've never gone for that. She glanced at the pages again. "It says here I'm supposed to tie him to a horse. What the hell? Why is there suddenly a horse in this movie, and why would I do that?"

Vince snickered. "I'm sure that means a bondage horse, Joy. Like a sawhorse, only padded and big enough for a human to drape themselves over it."

"Oh. Oh! That's… not where I saw this movie going," she said, her voice trailing off as she tried to understand why Finn wanted to go that direction. "I thought this was supposed to be an emotional flick, not slapstick. Because that's what this scene is going to turn into if you guys put me in that." She pointed to the skimpy outfit in his hands.

"It's just a little levity. If it doesn't work, I'm sure they'll reshoot it."

"Perfect. That's exactly what I wanted to hear. I'll get to make a fool out of myself twice," she grumbled as he guided her toward one of the dressing rooms.

"Relax, Joy. The sex scenes are usually shot with minimal crew for the actors' privacy. It won't be as big of a deal as you think."

Famous last words.

An hour later, Joy was standing on set, holding a whip and shivering as her boobs spilled out of the leather bra. Vince had taken pity on her and let her wear a pair of leather hot pants instead of the G-string, but she suspected that had more to do with her cellulite than concern about her modesty. Still, the outfit didn't leave much to the imagination, and she felt like a fool. Quinn, on the other hand, playing her love interest, was wearing nude briefs and nothing else. He was two hundred pounds of tanned muscle and dark hair.

Most women would watch the film just for this scene, she thought. But she wasn't one of them. The man was twenty years her junior, and lusting after a man who was about the same age as her oldest son just made her feel like a perv.

"Quinn, go ahead and lie down on the horse so you're facing up," Finn said. "Perfect. Yeah, slide down just a bit so you're centered in the frame. Just like that." Finn turned to Joy. "Are you ready?"

Joy swallowed hard and nodded.

"When I call action, kneel down in front of him and make a show of tying his wrists to the metal loops on the horse."

"Okay." Joy picked up the red silk ribbon Vince had given her and waited for the signal.

"And, action!" Finn called.

Joy took her time moving toward Quinn, swaying her hips and licking her lips like she was some sort of predator. Then when she reached him, she said, "Tell me what will drive you crazy."

Quinn looked up at her with smoldering heat in his eyes and said, "Tie me to this horse and ride me like a pony."

A bubble of absurd laughter got caught in her throat, and she did her best to swallow it down.

But when he added, "Don't forget to whip me hard when I'm a bad boy," the laughter slipped out. She coughed, trying to cover it, but it was no use.

Finn heaved a giant sigh and said, "Try to be professional, Joy. We don't have all day."

"Sorry. I've got it now," she said, mortified that she couldn't keep it together. But really, how was she supposed to remain composed when they'd put her in a soft porn scene?

"Start at the beginning," Finn ordered.

Joy got up and moved to her mark. When he called 'Action' they repeated the scene. Joy continued to demand direction from Quinn as she portrayed an awkward dominatrix. Finally, the scene ended when she tripped over him and they knocked heads, resulting in them sitting against the sawhorse, groaning in pain.

"Cut!" Finn called and frowned at them with his hands on his hips. "I don't think that scene is going to work."

"Sorry," Joy said. "I can try to sex it up if you want."

He jerked back as if he'd been smacked. "God, no. We don't need to see that again."

"It truly was horrifying, wasn't it?" Prissy said as she appeared from behind the cameras. "You can't really blame Quinn though. I'm sure it's hard to get into character when you're supposed to be sexing a mom-type." She gave Joy a sickeningly sweet smile and passed her a muffin from the craft table. "I thought you could use a pick me up after embarrassing yourself like that."

Joy scowled at her but said nothing as she put the muffin down on the sawhorse and wrapped herself in her robe. She turned to the director. "Are we done for the day?"

"You and Quinn are. We'll rework the seduction scene to something less... cringeworthy." He nodded at Prissy. "Are you and Carly ready for the beach scene?"

"I am. Carly is probably still in the makeup tent. You know how it always takes them a little longer to get her ready. It happens when actresses start to age."

Joy wanted to smack her upside the head. The woman was

just so bitchy for no reason at all, other than her own insecurities.

"Oh, Joy," Prissy called over her shoulder as she walked off with the director.

Joy raised an eyebrow at her in question.

"Tell Troy I really enjoyed seeing him at my party and that I can't wait to take him up on that offer for private photos." She waved her fingers and bounced away with Finn.

A low growl came from deep in Joy's throat, causing Quinn to let out a chuckle. She glared at him. "Got something to say?"

He held his hands up in a stop motion. "Nope. Nothing other than wow, Prissy has balls. I would think twice about crossing you if I were her."

"You would?" she asked, confused. Joy was fierce in her convictions, but it wasn't as if she was going to throw down with a costar.

"Yep. Because if she pushes you too far, I'm willing to bet you'll find a way to take her down, and it won't be with petty comments."

Joy shook her head. "I have no interest in feuding with her. I just want to make this film and move on."

He pulled a robe on and then picked up the muffin she'd left on the horse. "That's big of you." Holding up the muffin, he asked, "Were you going to eat this?"

She shook her head. "It's all yours."

"Thanks. And by the way, you were great in this scene."

Joy groaned. "You're delusional. I was awkward and completely out of my comfort zone," she said.

"You were supposed to be. That was the scene, and you played it brilliantly." He took a bite of the muffin and then continued, "The scene didn't work because that's not your character. It was a bad rewrite. Don't worry about it. The next one will go better."

"That was... thank you, Quinn. That makes me feel better." She turned to leave, ready to be anywhere other than on the set. But she paused and turned around when she heard what she thought was gagging.

Quinn was bent over a trash bucket, vomiting. Joy's stomach rolled with sympathy, and she had to take a step back just so she wouldn't be joining him over the trash. When he straightened, his face was white and there was a sheen of sweat on his forehead.

"Oh my god, Quinn. Are you all right?"

He pressed a hand to his stomach and shook his head slightly. "I think it was the muffin."

They both turned and stared at the half-eaten muffin that was back on the sawhorse.

The muffin that Prissy had brought her.

"Quinn?" she asked.

"Yeah?" He was clutching a bottle of water that had been on the small craft service table.

"Has Prissy ever brought you food or coffee before?"

"No." His body jerked as if he was going to vomit again.

"Hmm. Interesting." Images of Prissy bringing Joy coffee, the muffin, and even the pink drink at the party flashed through her mind. After each one, she'd suffered some minor malady. Well, Quinn reaped the consequences of the muffin, but Joy had experienced a breakout and a mysterious sore throat. Was it possible her costar was sabotaging her? Yes, yes it was. And it was time Joy put a stop to it.

CHAPTER NINETEEN

*a*fter Joy changed out of her dominatrix outfit and into a pair of jeans and a sweatshirt, she hightailed it back to the trailer she was now sharing with Prissy. Because Prissy was filming down at the beach, Joy had the place to herself and quickly started rummaging through all the drawers and cabinets, looking for anything incriminating that would help to prove Prissy was hexing Joy with childish ailments.

When Joy didn't find anything in the main room, she moved to the dressing room area and grimaced at the mess Prissy had made. Clothes were strewn all over, with dirty underwear hanging out on the floor. "Classy," Joy muttered and stepped over the offending garment. After rummaging through several of the drawers, she opened the one closest to the floor and grimaced. There was a pile of condoms, lube, and what appeared to be edible underwear. Joy was just about to shut the drawer when a tin with a pentagram drawn on top caught her eye.

She reached in gingerly and pulled it out. The tin was black with a skull and crossbones on it that said, *Get Out of Work Free*

Spells. The fine print read: *Need an excuse to call in sick? Don't let needing a doctor's note stop you. Just take a GOWFS pill and wait for your illness to appear. Lasts for up to 32 hours.*

"Gotcha!" Joy cried. She shoved the tin into the front pocket of her sweatshirt and hurried back into the main section of the trailer. She pulled the front door open and stared right into the face of her arch nemesis.

"Got what?" Prissy asked, eyeing her with suspicion. "If you stole the blunt in the cookie jar, things are going to get ugly."

"Blunt? What?" Joy asked.

"Oh, for the love of the goddess," she groused. "Just how uncool are you?"

"Very," Joy confirmed. "Now if you'll excuse me, I have somewhere to be."

"Whatever." Prissy waved a hand and flopped into one of the chairs.

Joy knew she should've just left, but she couldn't help asking, "Why are you here? Aren't you supposed to be filming?"

"Carly needed some time," she said with a shrug. "Whatever. I could use a nap." Her eyes narrowed as she studied Joy. "How are you feeling? You look a little green around the edges."

"Do I?" Joy asked. She shrugged. "Must be the lighting. I feel fine."

"Did you… um, eat today?"

"Yep," she lied. "Great muffin. Thanks."

"Huh. Okay. Well, see you tomorrow." She studied her nails as if her manicure was the most interesting thing on the planet, but she kept casting suspicious glances at Joy.

"Later." Joy bounded out of the trailer and ran straight into Detective Coolidge. "Oomph."

The detective reached out and caught Joy by the arms, keeping her from stumbling sideways. "Careful."

"Sorry," Joy said, stepping back to regain her balance. "Can I help you with something?"

"Yes, you can," the detective said coolly. "I'm going to need you to come down to the station for questioning."

"About my visions?" Joy asked.

"You could say that." Coolidge pulled out her cuffs, quickly secured Joy's arms behind her back, and said, "You have the right to remain silent—"

"Silent about what?" Joy gasped out. "What is it I'm being arrested for?"

Before the detective could answer, Carly appeared. "What the hell is going on here?" she demanded in a tone that was so full of anger that Joy almost hadn't recognized her voice.

"Joy Lansing is under arrest for obstruction of justice," Coolidge said.

"What? You've got to be joking," Joy said out of pure disbelief.

"Joy, don't say one word to her," Carly ordered. "Do you hear me? Not one word. I'll get my lawyer, and we'll get you out as soon as possible."

"I don't—" Joy started, but Carly cut her off.

"No. Not one word. It's clear they're building a case against you because they can't run down any leads."

"All right," Joy said, anxiety crawling all over her skin. Was she really being arrested? Was this real life? Why in the world did the detective think she had anything to do with the abduction of Carly's niece? Fear settled in her gut, and her head started to spin.

"Oh. My. God," Prissy said. "Of course, you're a criminal. I knew that goody-two-shoes garbage was just an act."

"You're calling me a criminal?" Joy cried, finally letting the stress of the day overwhelm her. "You're the one who has been poisoning my food and drinks with hexes to curse my skin or make me sick. What is wrong with you? Do you need meds? Who the hell does that?"

"Me?" Prissy asked, placing a hand on her chest as if she were in shock. "What makes you think I'd do something like that?"

"Because I found your stash in your sex drawer," Joy said coldly. "It's in my sweatshirt pocket."

"Thief!" Prissy said as she walked right up to Joy and reached for her pocket.

Detective Coolidge stepped right in front of her. "You need to step back, Miss. This is official police business."

"She has my gag spells. She stole them!" Prissy shouted. "Arrest her!"

"Okay, that's enough, Prissy," Finn Chance said as he walked into the commotion. He stared at Prissy. "Go to your trailer. Now."

Prissy let out a huff and stormed back inside.

He turned around and scanned Joy, his eyes landing on the handcuffs. "You can't arrest my actress," he said to the detective. "Whatever you think she did, you're wrong. She's the most honorable person on this set. If you haul her in, it will be all over the tabloids, and when you have to admit you were wrong, your entire department will be a joke."

Coolidge ignored him and pushed Joy forward toward the cruiser that was parked at the front of the lot. Joy glanced back and stumbled, nearly falling to her knees, but Coolidge had a decent grip on her arm and steadied her.

"Don't say anything, Joy! Not one word," Carly called again.

"She seems pretty insistent that you don't talk to us,"

Coolidge said conversationally.

Joy grunted.

"Nothing to say, huh? I doubt that's going to help you, considering the evidence we have, but go ahead and keep your mouth shut. We'll just find out what a judge has to say. You should be arraigned within, oh, seventy-two hours or so."

"Seventy-two hours! You can't be serious," Joy said.

"Very." The detective yanked the back door of her cruiser open and shoved Joy in. Just as Joy's rear hit the seat, a flash went off in her face, and she winced. Perfect. It would only take a couple hours before that hit the tabloids. Her life had morphed from quiet anonymity to mysterious model to hot-mess actress in the matter of just a few months. If she managed to avoid jail, the likelihood of anyone hiring her again was probably less than zero. She leaned back into the seat, winced at the pain in her wrists, and closed her eyes. Maybe when she opened them, the nightmare would be over.

* * *

COOLIDGE SAT across from Joy in the same conference room they'd sat in the week before. The detective leaned in and pushed two photos toward her. "Want to tell us what these are, Ms. Lansing?"

Joy glanced down at the two drawings she'd made of her visions. One was the house and the other was the man holding Harlow. Neither were the originals. They looked like computer prints. How had they gotten her drawings? Joy glanced up at her and said nothing.

"Isn't it true that you've been having visions this entire time but decided not to tell us the details?" Coolidge pressed.

No. That wasn't true at all. But Joy was hesitant to say

anything. If she told Coolidge that Carly had said she'd talk to them, would Carly be in trouble since she clearly wasn't their source?

"Who is this man?" The detective pointed at the picture in front of her. When Joy didn't answer, Coolidge pressed on. "Where is this house, and why did you draw it?"

When Joy continued to remain silent, Coolidge tried to appeal to her motherly instincts. "We can do this all day, Ms. Lansing, but I'm sure you have a home life to get back to. A son who just broke his leg and likely needs help?"

Joy narrowed her eyes at the detective and thought, *what a manipulative bitch.* "I want my lawyer. I'm not answering anything until I have representation, especially since it looks as if you've been poking your nose into my personal life."

Coolidge sat back and crossed her arms over her chest. "You do realize that your entire life is being detailed in the *Premonition Perspective*, right?"

Son of a... of course it was. Kyle's accident had been covered as a reckless kid who'd run away from home after coming out to his father. "So you thought it was a good idea to use my son's injury to get me to say something? That's low, Detective."

The door banged open and a tall dark-haired man with muscles piled on muscles stared at Coolidge and barked, "My office. Now!"

"But sir—"

"Shut up, Coolidge. If you don't, I'll fire you on the spot." Without another word, the chief of police turned and stormed out, clearly expecting her to obey his command.

Another man walked in, this one in an expensive three-piece suit. He was carrying a briefcase and had a kind smile. "Joy Lansing?"

She nodded.

"I'm your lawyer. Carly Preston sent me. Are you ready to get out of here?"

"Yes. Is that allowed?" she asked, her heart racing with anticipation. They hadn't actually booked her. Coolidge had just marched her into the conference room and then proceeded to interrogate her about something that Joy knew was complete bullshit. She couldn't be compelled to tell the police about her visions. That wasn't obstruction of justice. They'd have to put her on the stand to force her to talk.

"It is allowed. I've spoken with the chief and he agrees that they don't have any grounds to keep you."

"Oh, thank the heavens." Joy stood up, and glanced over her shoulder at her still-cuffed wrists. "I think we're going to need some help."

"I've got this," a young police officer in uniform said as he hurried in and quickly freed her. "I'm sorry you had to go through this, Ms. Lansing."

She let out a grunt and nodded. "Thanks."

"Do you think... um, do you think I could get an autograph?" he asked nervously, holding out a napkin.

Joy hesitated and then looked at the lawyer. All she wanted to do was leave, but this was the first time anyone had asked for her autograph and she didn't want to say no. She wanted this memory to help blot out the righteous anger she'd felt for most of the afternoon.

Her attorney nodded once.

"Sure," Joy said to the young officer and took the napkin. She sat back down at the table and started to write a quick note, but then her world went black. When it cleared again, she saw Carly standing in front of the large Victorian house where Harlow was being held. And Baldy was with her.

CHAPTER TWENTY

"Ms. Preston asked me to relay the message that she will call you this evening," the lawyer said as he walked Joy out of the station. There was a crowd of photographers across the street who suddenly perked up and started taking picture after picture. Joy wanted to scream when she saw them there. Didn't they have any better stories to chase? Though she supposed her arrest was going to get a lot of clicks. At least they were on the other side of the road. She imagined there was some rule requiring them to stay a certain distance away from the station, otherwise they'd be all up in her face like normal.

Joy stared up at the polished man, still reeling from her vision. When she'd come to at the conference table, she'd been breathing hard and her heart was racing, and she had a bone-deep sense that she needed to keep her vision to herself. "Do you know where she is?"

He shook his head. "Her message was short. She asked that I come get you out of here and said she'd call you as soon as possible. Do you need a ride somewhere?"

"Yes, I—" A silver Lexus that was going way too fast swung into the parking lot and came to a stop right in front of them. Joy's blood pressure eased slightly as she spotted Gigi climbing out of the car.

"Joy! Thank the gods. Are you all right?" Gigi wrapped Joy in a hug and held on tight and whispered, "Who is this goon? Do I need to get rid of him?"

"He's fine," Joy said with a relieved chuckle. "But thanks for having my back."

Gigi let her go and said, "Anytime." Then she turned to the lawyer and held her hand out. "Hello, I'm Gigi Martin. Joy's friend."

"Sebastian Knight. Joy's lawyer." He shook her hand and held it, seeming resistant to let it go.

Gigi let out a tiny gasp and stared up at him with wide eyes. Then she whispered, "Sebastian? Is that really you?"

He nodded slowly, his gaze roaming all over her, and then he suddenly dropped her hand and took a step back. "It's been a very long time, Clarity."

Clarity? Joy thought. Where had that come from?

Gigi cleared her throat. "I go by Gigi now. And it's been way too long. I can't believe I didn't recognize you." Her smile turned soft as she added, "It's the hair… and the suit. I don't think I've ever seen you in anything other than jeans and a concert T-shirt."

His lips twitched. "High school seems like a lifetime ago." His phone buzzed, and he said, "Excuse me."

Joy stared at Gigi and mouthed, *He's hot!*

Gigi gave her a look that said *not now* and turned back to Sebastian, who was tucking his phone away.

"I've got to go," Sebastian said, smoothing his tie. "Work emergency."

"That's too bad," Gigi said. "How long will you be in town? Do you think we can grab dinner and catch up?"

His eyes lit with interest, but then just as quickly, the interest vanished and was replaced by regret. "Sorry. I'm headed to the airport now. But it was really nice to see you again, Clarity—I mean, Gigi." He took a step forward, his arms slightly apart as if he were going to hug her, but then he took a step back and shook his head. "Gotta go." He glanced at Joy and quickly handed her a business card. "Call me if you run into any more issues."

Then he strode across the parking lot, climbed into a gray Toyota, and was gone.

Joy cleared her throat. "Old boyfriend?"

Gigi pressed a hand on her chest, and while still staring in the direction his car had gone, she said, "Something like that."

Joy let out a low whistle. "There's definitely a story there."

With a sigh, Gigi nodded and said, "Let's go. Everyone is freaking out."

"They are? About me being arrested?" Joy closed her eyes and shook her head. "How bad is the press?"

"Let's just put it this way," Gigi said, pulling the driver's side door open. "The headlines are speculating how long your prison sentence will be."

"I should've known," Joy said with a groan.

"Come on." Gigi waved for her to get in the car. "It's time for a coven meeting."

"Not today. There's somewhere else we need to go." Joy hurried over to the passenger side and got in.

"Where's that?" Gigi put the car in gear and headed out of the parking lot.

"Carly Preston's house. I have questions, and they can't wait."

* * *

As it turned out, Joy didn't have any choice but to wait for her questions to be answered. Carly's house was dark, and no one was home. She wasn't answering her phone either, even though it had been a few hours since she'd left the station and Carly had relayed her the message that she'd call that evening. But even so, Joy was willing to camp out all night if she had to. One way or another, she was getting answers about her vision.

"Joy," Gigi said patiently. "We look like stalkers. You don't want this to get out to the press, do you? Maybe we should go get something to eat and then come back?"

"If they haven't noticed us yet, I doubt they're going to." Joy peered at the handful of photographers across the street from Carly's house. They'd parked behind a van when they'd first arrived, shielding them from view. The van had since left, exposing the silver car, but so far no one had realized they were there.

Gigi sighed. "What if I need to use the bathroom?"

"Do you?" Joy asked.

"No. But I will eventually."

"We'll worry about it then."

Gigi opened her mouth to argue, but a black SUV shot past them and whipped into Carly's driveway.

Joy said, "That's our cue. Come on." Without waiting for Gigi's reply, Joy scrambled out of the car and peered through the darkness up the street. The photographers were in a frenzy, trying to get a shot of Carly, and were unlikely to realize Joy and Gigi were there until they were right in front of the house. Perfect.

"All right, Murder She Wrote," Gigi grumbled. "Let's get this done."

Joy grinned at her. "You're a good sport."

"One for all and all for one or some shit like that, right?" Gigi said as she followed Joy up the street.

Joy had been right about the paparazzi. They had been taken off guard by her arrival, but they bounced back quickly, shouting out questions and accusations, wondering when her trial was going to be, if it was true that she'd assaulted Prissy Penderton, and why she wasn't at home taking care of her son instead of partying every night with no regard to his mental health.

"Holy shit, Joy," Gigi whispered as she clung to her arm. "Is it always like that?"

"It is lately. You'd think there was nothing more important going on in the world with the way they make up the stupidest gossip about me. I'm like the most boring woman on the planet. I don't get it."

Gigi let out a guffaw of laughter as they headed up the walk to Carly's house. "That's rich."

They came to a stop on the porch and rang the doorbell. While they waited, Joy gave her a bewildered look. "What does that mean?"

"Oh, Joy. Come on. You're a forty-eight-year-old woman who came out of nowhere with a national ad campaign that landed you a part in a movie with two high-profile actresses. And you're dating a famous photographer. Don't you realize that women everywhere are awed by the direction that your life has taken? Add in the fact that you have three beautiful, well-adjusted kids, and you're the envy of the town. Of course the gossip rags are going to write about you. You're the new Jennifer Aniston."

"That's ridiculous. I will never come close to being Jennifer Aniston. You're the one who needs to get a grip."

"Whatever." Gigi waved an unconcerned hand. "You get what I mean. The fact is, you've started over and excelled at an age when a lot of women are thinking that their best years might be behind them. You're a freaking inspiration. Embrace it, girlfriend. You deserve it."

Joy opened her mouth to deny her words but then closed it. Gigi made some good points, and from that perspective she could see why people might be fascinated with her life. Joy still thought the level of interest bordered on insanity, but she could at least be proud to be a role model. Only now she needed to do something about cleaning up her reputation. The gossip rags hadn't done her any favors in that department.

The door swung open, and Baldy barked, "What do you want?"

"I need to talk to Carly. I've had another vision," Joy said.

"Let her in." Carly's tired voice floated from behind him.

Baldy scowled but stepped aside. Joy walked in, but he moved in front of Gigi, stopping her. "Who are you?"

"That's Gigi. She's one of my coven sisters," Joy said. "You can trust her. She helped with the finding spell."

"Gary, stand down." Carly was sitting in one of her armchairs with a hand over her eyes. She looked completely exhausted.

"You know I'm just doing my job," he muttered but then begrudgingly disappeared into another room, leaving them alone with the actress.

"Joy, are you all right?" Carly asked without uncovering her eyes.

"Yes, but are you?" Joy sat in the chair next to her.

"No." She dropped her hand, revealing her tear-stained cheeks and bloodshot eyes. "Not really. But that's been the case ever since Harlow went missing."

"What happened at the house?" Joy asked.

Carly sat up, her entire body alert. "How did you know about the house? Wait, you had a vision, didn't you?"

Joy nodded.

"Was she there? Did you see Harlow?" Carly asked urgently.

"No. I just saw you and Baldy... I mean Gary, standing out front. That was it."

Carly's lips quirked the tiniest bit at the mention of Baldy, but the hint of a smile quickly vanished. "My private investigator found the house, and Gary and I went to bring her home. Only the house was empty. There were traces that someone had been there recently. Dishes were in the sink, and the radio was on." She slumped back into her chair. "I'm pretty sure they'd just left, and now we're out of leads."

"How did your PI find the house?" Joy asked. Grace had been working on it through the real estate archives, but so far, she hadn't had any luck at all.

"He traced a call to my phone and found the tower that picked it up. From there, he searched the area until he found the place."

That was a lot simpler than searching real estate, Joy thought. "Why didn't you tell the police?"

"That's... private." She glanced away and stared out the window, though there wasn't anything to see. It was dark and the moon wasn't even shining.

"You never told them about my visions, did you?" Joy asked.

Carly shook her head. "The ransom isn't just for money. They're threatening to release information about my niece that I can't risk getting out. If the police get ahold of it, there's no way it would remain private."

Stunned, Joy sat back in the chair. "It's that devastating to your niece?"

"Yes." Carly rose. "I'm tired. If you'll excuse me, I need to rest now."

"Carly?" Joy asked.

"Yes?"

"Do you know how the detective knew about my visions?"

"No. But I've asked Gary to look into it." She drifted up the stairs, leaving Joy and Gigi alone in her living room.

Gigi let out a low whistle. "Wow. That's a lot."

"Yeah." They sat there for a minute, and Joy couldn't help but wonder what information about Harlow was so awful that they couldn't risk the press finding out. Carly and her immediate family were already splashed all over the press. Joy would've thought their lives were already an open book. It just went to show that not everything was as it seemed.

"Don't you think it's time you two were on your way?" Baldy asked from his spot in the doorway of what looked to be a study.

Joy stared at him, trying to figure him out. "Who are you to Carly?"

"That's really none of your business, Ms. Lansing." He moved to the door and held it open for them. "Goodnight."

CHAPTER TWENTY-ONE

$\mathcal{C}$ ars were stacked four deep in Joy's driveway when Gigi dropped her off.

"Looks like you're having a party," Gigi said. "A welcome home from the clink celebration?" she teased. "If you include the paparazzi over there, you could call it a rave."

"I hope there's cake," Joy said, sagging in the passenger seat and eyeing the half dozen photographers camped out across the street. "I could use the sugar jolt."

Gigi reached over and patted her thigh. "I'm sure the amount of love waiting for you on the other side of that door will help." There was a wistfulness in her tone that caught Joy's attention.

"Yeah." Joy smiled, already knowing who she'd find inside her house. All three of her children, Jackson, and Troy. She hadn't spoken to Hunter much other than to fill him in on Kyle's injury, so to see his car parked out front sent her heart soaring. She wondered how Troy was fairing with them all, considering he was the new boyfriend. The thought was both a happy one and a little terrifying. If they decided they didn't like him, she was going to be crushed. She hadn't intended to jump into a relationship with the first man who came along, but she couldn't deny there was something between them. Something that, as much as she'd loved Paul, had never been present in her marriage. She eyed Gigi. "You know we're your family now, right?"

"Huh?" Gigi asked, appearing to be startled.

"Grace, Hope, and I. We're your family. That might not look like what's waiting for me inside, but it's true and powerful, and if and when you need us, we'll be there."

"Thanks, Joy." Gigi reached over and gave Joy a hug. "Now go on and stop worrying about me just because I'm having a moment of thinking about what could've been if I hadn't married a complete ass."

"It's not over, you know," Joy said as she pushed her door open. "If you want a nuclear family, there's still time to do something about that."

She chuckled. "You mean like a sperm bank or something? Nah. I don't think these eggs are gonna be up for it. You know what they say; once you hit forty…"

"Are you forty?" Joy asked, taking her in. She'd always thought Gigi was in her early thirties. If she was forty, she must've been drinking from the fountain of youth, because there wasn't a wrinkle in sight.

"Forty-one actually." She shrugged. "I know it's still possible. I'm just not sure it's the dream anymore."

"I hear you. I can't deny the fact that I'm enjoying my freedom now that mine are grown. Though it is nice when they still need me." Joy climbed out of the car. "Thanks, Gigi. See you later."

Joy watched her drive away and started to wonder about Gigi's past even as the photographers started circling. She ignored them as it occurred to her that she didn't know that much about her friend's life prior to coming to Premonition Pointe. She knew she'd had an abusive husband, and Gigi had stood up to him in a way that not only freed her from his clutches but also showed him she wasn't one to mess with. She'd magically kicked his ass and cemented herself as a badass witch in the eyes of the coven. Then she'd proven to be kind and gentle and a great friend, too. Joy hoped she'd learn her whole story one day.

Joy heard the chatter of her kids through an open window and smiled to herself. It was a sound she never got tired of hearing.

The door swung open and Britt walked onto the porch. "Mom? What are you doing out here? We've been waiting for you."

"I was just taking a breath." Joy wrapped an arm around her daughter's shoulders and the pair walked in together. "What's the occasion?"

Britt gaped at her. "What's the occasion? Are you serious? We're all waiting to find out how jail has changed you."

There was a collective laugh, and then Hunter strode over to her and wrapped her in a bear hug.

"Hey, baby," Joy said, burying her face in his shoulder. He was taller than his siblings and always made Joy feel like she was some sort of waif even though she was taller than average height. "How are you doing?"

He pulled back and stared down at her as he shook his head. "I'm good, Mom. But right now, I want to know about you. What happened today?"

She smiled at him. "I guess I was just dying for more attention, so I had to go and get myself arrested."

He rolled his eyes. "Funny. Care to tell us all what *really* happened?"

Joy gave a quick rundown of the events, including the fact that she'd been having visions, and asked them all to keep quiet about it for now. "The visions are irregular and only seem to be connected to this event. I'm not sure why it's happening, but it is. Carly has a PI working on any information I can give her, and I guess the detective wasn't thrilled. As it turns out, I didn't do anything wrong. And according to the lawyer, the arrest is pure harassment."

"That's so wrong," Kyle said with all the righteous indignation a twenty-two-year-old could muster.

Jackson, who was sitting next to Kyle, holding his hand, nodded his agreement.

It made Joy smile to see her son being open about his relationship with Jackson in front of everyone and for everyone to accept them without question.

"Hey," Troy said, moving to stand next to her. "I just came by to make sure you're all right. It appears you are, so I think I should take off and let you enjoy your kids."

Joy turned to him and frowned. "You think you should, or you just want to?"

He shoved his hands in his pockets and glanced around. "I don't want to intrude."

"You're not intruding," she insisted. "In fact, if you're up for it, I'd love for you to get to know my kids a bit. They're great. But if you'd rather not or have other plans, that's okay too."

"I like your kids," he said, his lips curving into a wide smile. "They're funny and have already told me a bunch of embarrassing stories about you. I keep wondering how much more I can pry out of them before the evening is over."

Joy chuckled. "Oh, I bet it won't take much."

It wasn't long before they all moved to the dining room where there was Chinese takeout waiting. The loud, raucous group ate, drank, and told stories until everyone was smiling and satisfied. It was a rare moment that Joy cherished. Her kids were so busy moving on with their lives, it wasn't often they were all able to be together. She didn't want to see it end.

But eventually, Hunter and Britt cleared the table and proceeded to clean up while Jackson helped Kyle to his room, leaving Joy and Troy alone.

"This was an evening I didn't know I needed," Troy said, smiling softly at her.

"What? You don't put on your dating profile that you're looking for a woman with three snarky twentysomethings who are mostly self-absorbed but do eventually decide it's time to check on their mother?"

"No. Not exactly. But if I'd known it might attract you, I would've."

The smolder in his eyes did things to Joy, and she leaned into him as if she were stuck in his force field. His lips came down on hers, and it wasn't long before she was completely lost in his kiss.

"Um, oops," Britt said. "Sorry for interrupting."

Joy jerked back and felt her face flush with heat. "Hey, honey. Troy and I were just... well, I guess we were—"

Britt laughed. "I think it's pretty clear what you were doing."

Troy grinned at Joy. "There's no backpedaling now."

"Who's backpedaling?" Joy asked, straightening up and trying to shake off her embarrassment. "Did you need something, Britt? Can I help with the dishes or dessert or something?"

Britt clasped her hands together and had a nervous energy

about her as she said, "Hunter is finishing the dishes, and we didn't get dessert, but I'd very much like it if we could go out back and talk for a bit."

"Of course." Joy rose to her feet and asked Troy, "Wait for me before you go?"

"Sure. I'll be in the living room prying more stories out of Hunter."

Her insides warmed at the image, and she chuckled. "You two are gonna be trouble; I can tell."

He winked at her, and then Joy followed her daughter out onto the back patio.

"What's up, Britt?" Joy asked, wrapping her arms around herself when the breeze caused gooseflesh to pop out on her skin.

Britt moved to the large firepit, leaned down and lit a fire starter log, and then gestured for Joy to sit on the swing with her.

Joy did as she was asked and then just waited. Her daughter would speak when she was good and ready.

"I've made a decision," Britt said, staring at the fire.

"Okay. That's good."

Her daughter turned to stare Joy in the eye. "Is it? How can you tell? You don't even know what decision I've made."

"It doesn't matter if I know," Joy said with a shrug. "All that matters is whether you're good with it and if it's the right choice for you." She knew this had to be about her boyfriend and the move to Texas, and while Joy desperately didn't want her daughter to move, if that was the decision she'd made, Joy would be supportive. She had to be or risk putting their close relationship in jeopardy.

"I spoke to my boss, and it turns out our company has a sister office in Austin," Britt said.

"Oh? Does that interest you?" Joy asked, already knowing the answer.

"Mom." She rolled her eyes, making Joy chuckle. "I think this is a way to give it a try with Dave. We talked today and worked some things out. I didn't realize just how unhappy he'd been with his job, and he apologized for the way he handled it. He said that if I didn't want to go that he really wanted to try long distance because he thinks we're the real deal, but he doesn't want either of us to give up our dreams."

Joy nodded. "That sounds like he's saying the right things. Does he mean it?"

She nodded. "I think he really does. And after giving it a few days, I realized that I'm not ready to give up on us either. So I'm going to move to Texas and see what happens. If it's not right, I can come home and probably have a job waiting for me. But if I don't go, I'm always going to wonder."

"Just as long as you're sure, Britt. If you are, I'll support you a thousand percent."

"But?" she asked. "I can hear that but in there. You know that, right?"

Joy chuckled. "Wrong. There's no but. I'll always be here to support you. I just want you to make sure that he respects you and your career just as much as he does his. If he thinks his ambition takes precedent, then you two still have stuff to work through. Because Britt, your wants and needs are just as important as his. Don't ever take a backseat to a man because his ego is bruised. Okay?"

She nodded solemnly. "I hear you, Mom. And thank you." Britt wrapped her arms around Joy and hugged her for a very long time.

"When are you going?" Joy asked, doing her best to hold back tears.

"Next month." There was a catch in her daughter's voice, and that was the end of Joy's stoicism. The tears spilled unchecked down her cheeks, and when they finally pulled apart, they shared watery smiles as they laughed at each other.

"Come on, kid," Joy said, standing. "Let's go inside. We deserve ice cream."

"We have ice cream?" she asked, and her eyes lit up like those of the little girl she'd once been.

"Of course we do. I'll show you where I keep my secret stash."

Five minutes later, with ice cream in their hands, the pair went into the living room. Hunter made noise about getting his own ice cream, while Britt retreated to one of the bedrooms to call Dave.

Joy sat down next to Troy on the couch. "I love these kinds of nights. There's nothing better than spending a fun night with my kids. But I'd be lying if I said I didn't enjoy this right here. The quiet after the storm. My heart is full, and my world is just right." She glanced up at Troy. "Do you know what I mean?"

"I think so. It's that peaceful moment of gratitude for life and love."

Joy's heart swelled, and she nearly had to hold back her tears again. "That was perfectly put."

He reached out and caught the one tear that had escaped and then brushed his thumb over her cheek. "Is everything all right with Britt?"

"Yeah. She's moving to Texas. I'm going to miss her terribly." She gave him a wobbly smile but was proud she hadn't broken down in tears again.

"You'll visit," he said and pressed a soft kiss to her lips.

"Definitely. At least she'll be away from the damn paparazzi."

"Always looking on the bright side." He tucked her in close to his side and spent the next half hour cuddling her and caressing her arm. She settled against him, loving the way she felt wrapped up in him. Eventually, the soothing caresses started to make her skin tingle, and she couldn't stop herself when she palmed both of his cheeks and gave him a heated kiss. When they pulled apart, they were both breathing heavily.

"We should take this to my bedroom," she said, tracing a finger along his jawline.

Troy closed his eyes, obviously reveling in her touch. "Are you sure? I don't want anything to be awkward with your kids here."

She chuckled softly. "Troy, they are all adults. I'm certain they can handle it." She climbed out of his embrace and stood. Reaching down, she grabbed his hand and pulled him up and then down the hall to her bedroom. As soon as she shut and locked the door, all thoughts of her children fled, and for the next few hours, all of her attention was devoted to the kind, sexy man who made her feel desired and cherished. She knew that night, that no matter how new their relationship was, she wasn't letting him go. He was the one she wanted.

CHAPTER TWENTY-TWO

*J*oy had been relieved when the production assistant had called to say filming was being delayed. It turned out that Prissy had come down with a mysterious illness, and they wouldn't be filming until the following week. So Joy had used that time helping her daughter pack up her things and get ready for the move, playing cards with Kyle while he was laid up with his leg, and reconnecting with her coven.

The night before she had to go back to work, the four coven members had met at the bluff, and instead of conducting a ritual, they'd consumed three bottles of wine. And that was the reason Joy was back on the set with a raging hangover headache.

A knock sounded at her trailer, and the PA called, "Joy? We're ready for you on set."

"Coming." She hurriedly swallowed a couple of ibuprofen and then tried to arrange her face so that she didn't end up looking like she was going to hurl. Why had she waited until the day before she had to go back to work to drink her weight in wine?

She was an actress, right? She had this. With her head held high, she exited her trailer, squinted at the bright sun, and followed the PA down to the beach where she was filming with both Carly and Prissy. Carly, who was wrapped in a thick wool shawl, stood staring out at the crashing waves. Joy moved to stand beside her.

"How's it going?" Joy asked.

"Not great," Carly said, her expression completely blank. "We've hit a dead end. I fear we've blown our shot and now I'll never find her. Maybe I should've trusted that police detective."

"I don't think so," Joy said. "I just heard she's been put on administrative leave while they investigate her for unethical conduct."

Carly turned slowly and stared at Joy with wide eyes. "You can't be serious. How did you hear that?"

"Your lawyer called me this morning to let me know there wouldn't be any more trouble. Apparently, he put a legal aid on it, and they found out she'd been hacking my phone and that's how she got my drawings. She knew I'd been having visions but used those drawings as a reason to speculate that I was involved somehow. He suspects she was looking for a promotion since she'd been passed over three times in three years. Solving a big case like this would certainly help in that department."

Joy had been shocked when she'd gotten the call, having assumed the lawyer had only been there to help for that one day. But it appeared Carly only hired the best, and that's exactly what she'd gotten. Even though Joy had assumed the incident was over, she was relieved that now there was no question about it.

"That's…" She shook her head, looking disgusted. "I don't have words for this. I'm so sorry, Joy."

"It's not your fault. Thank you for sending Sebastian to represent me. I have no idea what would've happened if you hadn't sent the best."

She reached out and squeezed Joy's hand. "I'm glad he was able to help. The only reason you're in the middle of this is because of me. I don't think I could handle it if someone else was harmed trying to help me with this."

"Carly, you know none of this is your fault, right?" Joy tugged her a little to face her so that she could hold Carly's gaze. "I'd do anything to help you find your niece. I'm not okay knowing she's out there and there's nothing more I can do."

Carly nodded. "I know, and I appreciate that. My PI is still searching."

"You know if I see anything else, I'll let you know ASAP."

"Thanks," Carly said.

Joy had been spending a lot of time studying Harlow's picture. Nothing had come through since the day she'd last been at the police station. "I heard the Premonition Pointe police put a new detective on the case, but so far no one has contacted me."

"Me neither." Carly shoved her hands into her pockets and glanced up the beach. "It looks like they're ready for us."

They walked in silence up the beach to where the scene was taking place, and over the next four hours, Joy watched Carly transform from the stoic, worried aunt, to a vibrant grandmother who was full of life. The moment the director released them, she faded back into the worried aunt and walked off without a word.

"Damn," Joy said to no one in particular. "The talent that woman has is breathtaking."

"That's a fact," Quinn said, standing beside her with his arms folded over his chest. His eyes were narrowed as if he were studying her.

"The way she can turn it on when she needs to, even with everything she's going through, is inspiring," Joy added. "I hope someday I can be even half as good as she is."

He glanced over at her. "You're already great, Joy. There's no need to compare yourself to Carly. She's an excellent actress, but acting isn't everything."

Joy frowned at him. "What's that supposed to mean?"

"Nothing." He shrugged and then gave her a smirk. "Just that everyone has their own gifts." He walked off, leaving her staring after him, feeling uneasy.

It wasn't so much what he'd said, but how he'd said it that made her think Quinn might have a problem with Carly. But why? She couldn't for the life of her come up with one single reason. The wind picked up and chilled her as she made her way back to her trailer. Just as she was about to enter, she heard Prissy's high-pitched voice behind her.

"Hey, Joy."

Joy suppressed a groan and turned around. "Prissy. What's going on? Are you feeling better?"

"Yes. No thanks to you. I puked my guts up for five days straight."

"I'm sorry to hear that, but I'm not sure why it's my fault," Joy said.

"Don't think I don't know that you retaliated against me just because I pulled a few pranks on you," she said with a sniff. When she spoke again, her voice was full of venom. "So what if you got a little bit of acne or a sore throat? You don't spike your coworker's lunch with enough hexing pills to almost send her to the ER."

"I didn't do that," Joy said coldly. "You're the one who tried to make me sick. If I were you, I'd start looking around at who else I'd managed to piss off. But leave me out of it." She spun around, stalked into her trailer, and slammed the door behind her, determined to never give Prissy another second of her time.

"Hello, Joy."

Joy let out a gasp and nearly jumped right out of her skin when she spotted Quinn standing just to the left side of the door. "Holy hell, Quinn. What are you doing here? You scared the life out of me."

"Not yet." His lips curved into a diabolical smile. "But there's still time."

She took a step back, intending to bolt from the trailer, but she was too late. He flung a handful of white powder in her face, and she lost consciousness as she crumbled to the ground.

* * *

THE POUNDING in Joy's head was a steady beat that matched the rhythm of her heartbeat. Her back ached, and when she tried to roll over, something stopped her. She blinked, trying to clear away her blurry vision, and groaned when her stomach turned.

"Finally. Wake up, you lazy witch," someone growled.

"Who's that?" Joy asked, still trying and failing to focus.

"Who do you think it is?" Footsteps reverberated through the room until she felt the dip of the mattress.

The scent of ocean and pine washed over her. "Quinn?" she croaked out. "What happened?"

"You practically overdosed on a crushed sleeping pill. For god's sake, do you have zero tolerance to pharmaceuticals?"

"Pretty much." Joy wasn't a fan of anything that wasn't herbal and avoided it at all costs.

"Wake up. We have work to do," he ordered. The footsteps started again, the noise sending her headache into full-blown migraine territory.

"Stop, please," she begged. "My head is killing me."

"That's because you hit it on the counter on the way down. I have never seen such a lightweight in my entire life. You'll never make it in Hollywood. Someone would slip you a Mickey, and that would be the end of you. If I hadn't been there today and given you a taste of coke, who knows how long you'd have been out? Maybe even never woke up. It's sad really."

Mickey? Coke? Quinn had drugged her? She tried to sit upright but was tugged back down, and that's when she realized her hands were tied to the headboard and her ankles were tied together. There was no way she was going anywhere. She continued to blink rapidly until her vision finally cleared, and then she narrowed her gaze on Quinn, who was leaning back in a chair, eyeing her. His face was gaunt as if he'd just come off a bender, and his clothes were rumpled in a way she'd never seen before. He always looked put together, but in the tiny room in what appeared to be a roadside motel, he looked like a junkie who was desperate for his next score.

"Why, Quinn?" she croaked out as she tried to separate her feet and failed. "What do you want?"

"What do you think?" He waved a hand around the room.

"If Carly doesn't pay that ransom, this is what I have to look forward to from now on."

"Carly?" Horror filled her and this time when her stomach rolled, she twisted just in time to expel the contents of her stomach onto the floor. The ties rubbed on her wrists and she wondered if when she got out of there her skin was going to be rubbed raw.

"You're disgusting," he said, getting up and moving into the tiny bathroom. When he emerged, he threw a towel over her vomit and sat back down, leaning forward with his hands clasped. "I've tried everything I can think of to get Carly to pay up. I still have my ace in the hole, but I'd rather not use that. There's a cost in Hollywood when you spill your ex's secrets. Some directors are touchy about that kind of drama. But I'll still do it if the payout is big enough."

"Your ex? You dated Harlow?" she asked in horror.

Quinn raised one eyebrow. "Are you always this slow?"

Joy stared up at the yellowing ceiling and tried to collect her thoughts. He had shown her a picture of him with Carly and Harlow. But didn't Harlow have a boyfriend? Baldy was considering selling the story. What was his name?

Quinton.

Holy shit. She'd had the clues right in front of her the entire time. But how could she have known Harlow's ex was behind the abduction? Clearly, Carly hadn't known, or she'd have been looking into Quinn herself.

"What happened to you?" Joy asked him.

"What happened, she asks," he said in a mocking tone. "What didn't happen?" He got up and started pacing. "At first, everything was great. Harlow and I were happy. We spent all our time together, and I was even thinking of asking her to marry me. But then Carly decided that her niece needed more out of life than just following an actor around, so she convinced her to enroll in a music program and it was all downhill from there."

"What was downhill?" Joy asked. "Your relationship?"

"No. Don't be an idiot. Harlow loved me," he said, his chin raised as if he was god's gift to women everywhere. "My career went downhill. Once I wasn't seen with the niece of Hollywood's most beloved aunt all the time, casting directors couldn't be bothered. My roles were diminishing, and the press was non-existent. You really just have no idea how good you have it with the paps following you around everywhere. If they're talking about you, that means they want you. And that translates into jobs and cash."

"So this is all about revenge because Carly's advice caused your star to slip?" Joy asked incredulously.

"It's not revenge. It's survival!" he roared and then slammed his fist down on a rickety nightstand. It wobbled and then fell over, taking the cheap lamp with it. "No one can tolerate going from being one of the most sought-after, up-and-coming stars to an actor who can't get a role in a movie unless his friend demands he's hired before she signs on."

"Prissy?" Joy asked warily. "She's the one who recommended you?"

"Yeah. But only because I hooked her up with a reliable supplier." He shrugged as if taking drugs was a completely normal everyday thing. Maybe it was in Hollywood. There were certainly enough rumors about it. But so far on set, no one seemed to be high. No one but Quinn anyway.

She vaguely recalled him agreeing with her that Prissy was a major pain in the ass. And yet, Prissy was the reason he even had a job. Joy guessed there was no honor among users.

"So what now? Why am I here?" Joy asked, needing to get

down to business. "Are you going to ask for a ransom for me, too? If so, I gotta tell ya, no one I know has the kind of money it takes to make drugging and abducting someone worth it." Her headache was still pounding, but righteous indignation had kicked in, and Joy was ready to fight this asshole until she had her hands around his neck and was able to choke the daylights out of him.

How dare he drug her and tie her up to some seedy motel bed. Jackass.

"You're here to motivate Carly to do the right thing." He grabbed an open bottle of beer from the counter and took a long swig. "She has a kind heart. I know that cousin of hers has been keeping her from paying me, but now that someone else is in danger, she'll be more motivated."

"Cousin?" Joy asked, stupidly. Because who else could it be?

"Terry? Barry? Larry? I don't know. Something like that. The bald one. He's the guy they always call when they need someone to help them with a sensitive manner. Like a fixer of sorts."

"Gary," Joy mumbled.

"What?"

"Nothing." She tried to shake her head and thought better of it when the pain intensified.

"I know what you think of me, you know," he barked, suddenly angry.

"You do?" Joy was dying to tell him what an entitled piece of shit he was. That he was blaming women for his own shortcomings and that he deserved to become a D-list actor who could only get a job on a reality game show. But she was currently tied to a mattress that was probably crawling with bed bugs and was in no position to antagonize him. Instead, she kept her mouth shut and hoped he'd talk until he passed out. Maybe then she'd have a moment to try to free herself from the bindings.

"Do you think I'm an idiot?" he snarled. "You think I'm a loser. Someone who deserved to get dumped."

"Harlow broke up with you?"

His lip curled, and he had the look of a deranged serial killer. Maybe she was pushing him too far. She wanted to shrink back, but there was nowhere to go. "She dumped me. Through a text. Who does that shit?" He stomped around the room, knocking a chair over and kicking the nightstand that had collapsed. "That bitch owes me."

And there it was. How dare Harlow live her own life instead of catering to him and letting him sponge off her family connections. He was the worst kind of asshole, and as far as Joy was concerned, the earth could just open up and swallow him whole.

"So you're here to pressure Carly into paying me enough so that I can set myself up in the Hollywood Hills, drive a Tesla, and act like every other rich movie star out there. Once I'm living the life, the roles will be handed to me on a silver platter."

His delusion was so thick he was drowning in it. "You know it doesn't really work that way, right?" she said before she could stop herself.

"The hell it doesn't," he snarled at her. "No one breaks into the movie business the way you did, *Joy*. It takes years and connections and status. And here you are, playing at being an actress, just because some famous photographer took a liking to you and shot some decent photos. Trust me when I tell you that I'm positive this will be your last role. You'll be a one-hit wonder if you're lucky. But no one will book you." He scanned her body and shook his head. "You've already aged out. Unless you're a Carly Preston, the roles just aren't there. Get used to it, princess."

Joy wanted to laugh in his face. The acting was the fun part for her, and she knew she could probably get roles with the local playhouse. If she never got another job again, it would be fine with her. More than fine maybe. She really loved the process, but pretty much everything else meant nothing to her. The fame, the publicity, the parties. She had no interest in that. And she definitely could live without headlining in every gossip magazine on the supermarket shelves. "Message noted."

He snorted. "You think I'm shitting you. That's all right, Joy. I know the truth, and you'll know soon enough."

She closed her eyes, trying to stop the throbbing over her left eye, and prayed he'd be eaten by a colony of fire ants. Yes, that would make her very happy indeed. "Does Carly even know I'm here yet?"

"She should. My stepbrother made contact a few hours ago," he said, sounding pleased. "He reiterated we were ready to push the button on Harlow if they didn't send the money by midnight, and that you would be out of commission until the funds are transferred and we are safely out of town. Then I might consider letting them know where to find you. Or not, if you continue to be a bitch."

"What a charmer," she muttered.

"Keep it up, Lansing. I'm dying to see if you can float with your arms and feet tied together."

An image of her body floating face-down in a pool flashed in her mind, and that was the moment she stopped engaging and started to rack her brain for an incantation spell that could loosen the bindings of her restraints.

It was too bad the only spell she could think of was the one to summon fire. It might burn her restraints, but she'd end up a crispy critter in the process.

Dammit.

Quinn continued to rant and rave and pound on the furniture through the evening. Every inch of Joy ached, and she started to despair. If Carly didn't override Gary to pay Harlow's ransom, why in the world would she do it for Joy? Quinn's logic didn't make any sense to her, but then she supposed that a frustrated man who was high on who-knew-what probably didn't have the soundest reasoning.

The hours dragged on, and Joy drifted in and out of consciousness until at some point she heard scratching at the door. Her eyes popped open, and her body stiffened. Was it Quinn's stepbrother? Or some other shady character like one of his drug dealers? She had no idea, but there was no time to waste. She needed to get out of her restraints one way or another.

Quinn sat passed out in the chair next to the bed, and Joy fervently wished that the man's heart had given out. It was better than he deserved.

Joy tested both of her wrists, twisting and trying to move her hands together on the rod of the headboard. If she could just get them closer, she might be able to use her fingers to free herself.

The bed squeaked, and she imagined that if anyone was below them, they were being treated to what they likely thought were bedroom gymnastics. The very idea made Joy shudder in disgust. That was it. She had to get out of there. Using all of her strength, she yanked her right wrist toward her left, and when they slammed together, sending pain all the way to her shoulder, she let out a grunt.

Quinn stirred, and she froze.

But his restlessness didn't last long, and Joy went to work on worrying the knots at her wrists. It took a while, but eventually the tie started to loosen. But just when she was about to pull her left wrist out of the tie, a hard fist slammed right into her face.

CHAPTER TWENTY-THREE

*T*hree things happened all at once. Pain exploded in Joy's cheek; she reared up and kneed Quinn in the balls with both knees; and the door flew open with a crash.

"Get the hell off her, you slimy creep!" Grace ordered, her voice full of pure rage.

Quinn, who'd already suffered a massive blow to his junk, grabbed himself and rolled over onto the floor.

Immediately, a bright stream of magic materialized from the door and hit Quinn square in the chest. He vibrated under the onslaught of magic streaming into him, but when her coven sisters finally dropped the magic, the asshole who'd drugged Joy and tied her to a dirty motel room bed, was immobilized, staring blankly at the wall with both hands still clutching his balls.

"Joy!" Hope rushed over and quickly started undoing the rest of the restraints. "Oh my god, are you all right? Are you hurt?"

"Ugh." Joy groaned and rolled gingerly to her side. "Everything hurts. And I need a bathroom."

"We've got you." Hope started to wrap one of Joy's arms over her shoulders and in the next moment, Grace was there doing the same with the other arm.

"You're okay, sweetie," Grace said. "It's over now."

"Harlow?" Joy croaked out. "Did you find her?"

"We did," Hope said. "She's okay. Let's get you to the bathroom."

By the time the cops showed up, Joy was sitting outside on the cement steps with a bag of ice covering her face. Her head was still pounding, but at least she'd worked a few kinks out of her aching body.

"Ms. Lansing?" a short, dark-skinned woman in slacks and a button-down shirt squatted in front of her. "I'm Detective Danes, and I was assigned this case after Detective Coolidge was suspended. I understand you've been through a lot tonight and were previously mistreated by Coolidge, but I'm hoping you can help me out. Fill in some blanks for me so we can make sure we have all our ducks in a row and see to it that Mr. Redmond gets a nice long stay in the state penitentiary. Do you think you can do that for me?"

"Yeah," Joy said, because if there was anything she wanted out of this ordeal, it was for Quinton Redmond to have a nice long stay behind bars. "I can do that."

She reached out and squeezed Joy's hand lightly. "Thank you. It will be just a few minutes before I can take you back to the station."

"I don't want to go there," Joy said.

The detective blinked at her. "I'm sorry. You don't want to make your statement at the office?"

"No. The last two times I was there, it was less than pleasant." Joy took a sip of the water that Gigi had handed her and stared out at the flashing lights of the police vehicles.

"Come back to my house," a familiar voice said softly.

Joy looked up and spotted Carly holding onto a woman that could only be Harlow. Carly gave her a pained smile and said, "I'm so glad to see you, Joy. I'm so sorry for this ordeal."

"It's not your fault," Joy said. "I can't tell you how happy I am to see Harlow with you."

The young woman cast a glance at Joy but quickly buried her face in Carly's shoulder again.

"Me, too," Carly said, softly. "Me, too." She turned to Detective Danes. "I'm taking Harlow home. If you want to talk to her, you'll need to come to my home. My security guard will give you the address if you don't already have it. Joy and her friends are welcome there." Without another word, Carly guided her niece toward the SUV where Gary was waiting.

Joy squeezed Hope's hand. "Thank you."

"There's nothing to thank us for, love," Hope said softly. "We didn't do anything you wouldn't have done."

"How did you find me?" she asked.

"Angela," Hope said simply. "I swear, that woman is more useful than a cat."

"Angela?" the detective asked with her eyebrows raised.

Hope gave her a patient smile. "She's my mother, and she has a serious case of telepathy. Can't turn it off. Well, tonight when she was grocery shopping, she overheard asshat's partner in crime bitching about the motel and what a pain in the ass Harlow Preston is. So she followed him here and called me. I called in my coven, and the next thing you know, we're like Charlie's Angels, kicking ass and taking names."

Danes snorted. "Yes, I guess you were. All right. I'll meet you all at Carly Preston's house. Is that all right with you, Ms. Lansing?"

Joy nodded, knowing Carly wouldn't let the police get away

with any shenanigans. And likely her lawyer, Sebastian, was already on his way.

* * *

Joy had been answering questions for over an hour in Carly's study when Sebastian Knight walked in. He took a seat next to her in a matching leather chair and crossed his ankle over his knee. He winked at Joy and then turned his attention to Detective Danes.

"Hello." He held his hand out and introduced himself. "I'm the counsel for Joy Lansing, Gigi Martin, Hope Anderson, Grace Valentine, and of course Harlow Preston. From now on, no questions will be answered unless I'm present. Do we have an understanding?"

Danes nodded and then smirked. "None of your clients are under investigation, Mr. Knight."

"I was already aware of that, but given the treatment of Ms. Lansing in the past, we're covering all bases."

"Noted." Detective Danes went back to asking detailed questions about Joy's stay in the motel and everything she'd talked about with Quinn. By the time another hour had passed, Joy was so tired and in so much pain, she was ready to cry.

"I think that's enough for the evening," Sebastian said, making Joy wonder if the man was also 'cursed' with telepathy as Hope would call it. "My client has been through enough for one day. If you want to talk to her again, call my office and we'll arrange a meeting."

Danes nodded and stood. "You seem like a caring and competent lawyer, Mr. Knight. I commend you."

"Thank you," he said simply and then watched her walk out

of the room. He turned to Joy. "You did well. I think the information you gave her will be a tremendous help for their case."

"I hope so. But do they even need it? I mean, Harlow—"

He put a hand up, stopping her. "Harlow doesn't remember anything about her abduction. It's lucky you have that vision to go on record. She was drugged and then never saw Quinton where she was being held. Without you, the case could've very well fallen apart."

"Whoa. I had no idea," Joy said, cupping her sore cheek.

"That's already bruising. You should ask Clarity—I mean Gigi—for a salve. I'm sure she has something that will clear it right up." He gave her a kind smile and stood, offering her his hand.

"How well do you know Gigi?" she asked curiously. Joy had been asked so many questions that night, it seemed only fitting that she ask a few of her own, even if they weren't any of her business.

"We used to be friends a long time ago," he said simply. "People don't tend to change that much."

She mulled that over and then nodded. "You know, I think you're right."

They found her coven and Carly in the main living area. Carly was busy gushing over them and giving them superhero names. It made Joy smile and then wince at the ache in her jaw.

"Joy," Carly said softly when she spotted her. "How are you feeling?"

"Honestly? Every square inch of me is in pain. Do you have a painkiller potion around here?"

"I do. Follow me." She rose gracefully from the couch, and Joy followed her into a room that could only be called an apothecary. The place was filled with herbs, potions in a chilled cooler, and every kind of ingredient anyone would be looking for when trying to cast a spell.

"This room is fantastic," Joy said, her eyes wide with awe. "Do you spend a lot of time here?"

She nodded. "Mixing potions and herbal remedies relaxes me. It's what I do to unwind."

"This must've been a huge time investment for a place you're renting for a short period of time."

"It would be," Carly said with a nod. "But I decided a while ago that I'd like to stay here for a while. So I have a long-term lease. I'm kind of hoping the owner will sell to me, but so far I haven't convinced him."

"That's... wow. It's really good, Carly. I can see you here."

Carly reached into a cooler and handed her a glass bottle. "This should do the trick. It will also accelerate healing."

"I wish I'd known about this when Prissy was punking me with her hexing spells. I would've asked you for something that would knock some sense into her or send her to live on another planet."

"That sounds really wonderful," Carly said. "I bet she'd thrive on Venus. It's a good place for bitchy people." She grinned and added, "But in the meantime, I might have slipped something I could've sworn was just a mood stabilizer into her coffee. But as it turned out, that didn't work so well for her. It did give us a little time off from her BS though."

Joy let out a bark of laughter. "Oh, my. If I didn't love you before, I do now. That's priceless."

Carly's eyes twinkled for the first time since Harlow was abducted, and it made Joy swell with happiness. The woman was just infectious. It was no wonder she was a megastar. People couldn't help but be drawn in. "She deserved it."

They both laughed, and then silence fell between them. Finally, Joy cleared her throat. "Can I ask you something?"

"Of course."

"What's the deal with Baldy? I mean, Gary. Quinn said he was your cousin. But Hope heard him talking about selling Harlow's story, and I'm not really sure why he still works for you. I mean, I've heard of some crazy stuff family has tried to do to each other for money. Is he blackmailing you or something? Because if he is, let's just take him out with the trash like we've done with Quinn. I'm serious. We'll deal with him right now."

Carly threw her head back and laughed so hard she started to gasp for air.

"Uh, Carly? I think you need to breathe."

By the time the actress finally got herself under control, she had to wipe the tears off her cheeks. "Oh, my. That felt good. Thank you, Joy."

"You're welcome?" Joy said, making it sound like a question. "What exactly was so funny?"

"Gary *is* my cousin. He's definitely not blackmailing me. Nor would he ever. He's just about the only person I trust who has our backs when things go crazy in this business. That day when Hope heard him thinking about selling a story to the press, that was just his frustration rearing its ugly head. We actually suspected that Quinn was party to the abduction, but no amount of investigating him revealed anything useful. As we know now, he wasn't actually the one who took her or held her, but he was the mastermind behind it. Anyway, Gary thought if he sold a couple of stories about Quinn's prior drug use, more would come out and we could get a lead there. But I said it was too risky because he'd dated Harlow for long enough that she'd be thrown into the lion's den. She didn't deserve that. I was protecting her."

"But you told him you were the only reason he wasn't arrested. Why would he be arrested?" Joy asked.

Carly's lips twitched into a smirk. "You don't miss much, do you?"

Joy shrugged. "I was really upset and wanted to help."

"Thank you for that." Carly squeezed her hand. "That was all part of my act. I can't have one of my guards turning on me, can I?" She grinned. "Not many people know Gary is my cousin. I prefer for people to not know that. It's easier for him to move around in life without being the subject of tabloids. "

"And Quinn? How did you work with him if you suspected he had Harlow?"

Her smile vanished and was replaced with a scowl. "I'll tell you, Joy, it was not easy. It took about a month of Harlow dating him for me to realize what a user he was. It was imperative that I got her away from him. In fact, I did a happy dance the day she broke up with him."

Joy nodded. "I can see why."

"I don't know how he got cast in this movie, but if I had known before I signed on, there is no way I'd have accepted the role. No way at all. But I'm a pro, and how would it look if I threw a major temper tantrum because of a side character that I didn't even have to interact with much?"

"It's a dilemma for sure. But look on the bright side," Joy said happily.

"What's that?"

"He's likely not getting out of jail on bail since he's broke, but even if he does, I can't imagine the film won't recast him. So lucky me, I get to do another incredibly awkward sex scene with some kid who probably couldn't find his way around a woman's pleasure zone even if he had detailed instructions and a flashlight."

Carly collapsed in her chair and laughed until her eyes leaked again, and Joy decided that she'd make a major effort to keep Carly Preston laughing every day that she was in Premonition Pointe.

CHAPTER TWENTY-FOUR

"Good morning, beautiful," Troy said as he cuddled up next to Joy's naked body and nuzzled her neck.

"Morning," she mumbled as she gazed out his bedroom window at the crashing waves. It had been four weeks since the abduction, and since then her life had been eventful. Joy had shared a tearful goodbye with her daughter Britt and sent her off to Texas with a man who might or might not be good enough for her. Only time would tell if Dave could grow into the man Britt deserved. Joy hoped so. She really did, because she liked the guy and could see that Britt truly cared about him.

The movie had been delayed for two weeks while they found a new love interest for Joy. They'd also insisted that Joy go to counseling since she'd been drugged and abducted while on the set. She wasn't naïve. She knew it was just to protect them in case she had a breakdown. But as it turned out, it had really helped when the anxiety had caught up with her. She'd never been an anxious person before, but traumatic events really were triggers for mental health issues, just like everyone said they were. The counseling was helping, and Joy was still going one day a week, just to keep everything in check since she'd gone back to work. The paparazzi, while still present, had found other more interesting people to write about, so Joy's name wasn't the talk of the town anymore.

That honor belonged to Harlow. It wasn't long after she came home that she decided it was time to tell her story. So Carly had called a trusted reporter, and the story had been published a week ago. In it, Harlow detailed the events of her father's death and her mother's role in the aftermath. It turned out that ten-year-old Harlow had walked in on her father choking her mother. There'd been a gun on the dresser, and Harlow used it to save her mom. Then when it was all over, Harlow's mom lied to cover for her daughter. She didn't want her little girl to be known as the child who killed her father. It was a major trauma for Harlow, and she'd been estranged from her mother and in therapy for years over it. Carly hadn't wanted her to do it, but Harlow insisted it was part of her recovery, and so far, she was handling it well. Even the press was mostly being respectful for the time being and leaving the Prestons alone. That didn't stop them from publishing stories, but that was to be expected.

"I was thinking breakfast in bed," Troy said as he ran his hand up the side of her body.

Joy shivered slightly, but it wasn't from being cold. "Who's making this breakfast?"

He chuckled. "Not you."

Joy rolled over and pressed a soft kiss to his lips. "Then that sounds wonderful. But I think I'm hungry for something else first."

They took their time making love to each other with the soundtrack of the ocean crashing against the rocks playing in the background. The past month with Troy had been everything she'd ever dreamed a relationship could be. They spent most nights together at either his place or hers. She was quickly becoming a huge fan of his, though. There was nothing more soothing than falling asleep and waking up to the sound and smell of the ocean.

Life with Troy was just fun. He was attentive and supportive and made her feel beautiful every day. And he was an excellent cook. It didn't hurt that all of her children liked him.

After their morning love fest, Troy disappeared into the kitchen, and when he returned, he handed Joy a tray with a goat cheese omelet, fresh berries, bacon, and a large cup of coffee.

"You've already gotten me into bed," she teased. "What's with the full-court press?"

He chuckled and climbed back onto the bed with her and stole a piece of her bacon. She'd also learned from all their sleepovers that Troy wasn't much of a breakfast eater. So the fact that he'd made it just for her was really pretty sweet. Or he wanted something. She decided both were probably true. Troy smoothed a lock of her hair behind her ear and said, "I was hoping you were free tonight."

"Sure. Aren't I always?" She took a long sip of her coffee.

"Not when you have a coven meeting," he said.

"Oh, that's true. Nothing stands in the way of time with my girls."

"Don't I know it," he said with a smirk. "Heaven help the man that gets between a witch and her coven."

"You said it, not me." She held her bacon out to him, offering him a bite.

He took it and then snatched the entire piece. "Damn, that's good."

"Yes, my compliments to the chef. Now, what are we doing tonight?" she asked.

"It's a surprise. Be ready at seven." He crawled out of bed and headed to the shower.

Joy watched him go, eyeing his round backside with appreciation. "What do I wear?"

"That sexy red dress in your closet."

"What sexy red dress?" she called back. But it was too late. The sound of water rushing through the pipes, followed by the squeak of the shower door, indicated that the conversation was over for the moment. And by the time he returned to the bedroom, Joy was so invested in her breakfast that she completely forgot about the mysterious red dress.

KYLE LET out a low whistle as Joy strolled out of her bedroom wearing the halter top dress that showed just enough cleavage but not so much that she was in danger of a wardrobe malfunction. It was knee-length and did wonders for showing off her toned legs. It was a dress that Joy would've instantly loved but might not have tried for fear she was a little too old for such a look. But, whoa, when she'd looked at herself in the mirror, that assessment would've been way off. Way, way off, because the sexy red dress was now her favorite item of clothing. In fact, she was considering wearing it daily, just so when she looked in the mirror, she saw the dress that did wonders for her minimal curves. It truly was a miracle.

"Where are you headed tonight?" Jackson asked from his spot on the couch. Kyle was sitting sideways with his legs draped over Jackson, and Jackson was busy running his hand through Kyle's thick locks.

"I have no idea. Troy just told me to be ready by seven and to wear this dress." She gazed at them and smiled. 'You two look awfully cozy tonight."

Kyle flushed while Jackson chuckled.

"Is it a special occasion?" she guessed.

Her son's face turned an even deeper shade of red, and Joy couldn't help but laugh.

"Okay, keep it to yourselves. And have fun while I'm out. Just be careful of the leg and remember to be safe. Got it?"

"Got it," they both said and saluted her.

She rolled her eyes and then averted her attention when the doorbell rang. Joy opened it to find Troy in a perfectly tailored black suit and red tie. He was holding a bouquet of red roses and a bottle of champagne. "Wow. You're really laying on the charm, aren't you?" she said by way of greeting.

"Sort of. The flowers are for you. The champagne is for those two." He nodded toward Kyle and Jackson and then placed the bottle on the table.

Kyle was so red he was almost purple now. Jackson whispered something in his ear that made Kyle choke out, "No! Don't you even think about it."

"Oh, please. I already know," Joy said. "It's so obvious by the way you're acting that you might as well write *hookup anniversary* on your foreheads."

Kyle stared at anything other than his mother while Jackson gave her a thumbs-up.

She chuckled while she took the roses into the kitchen and got them situated in a vase. When she was done, she breezed back into the living room, slipped her arm through Troy's, and on their way out, she called, "I love you both. Don't forget to be safe. There's a new box of condoms in the bathroom cabinet."

The front door shut, and Troy snickered. "I bet that's going to be a mood killer."

"I do what I can." Joy flipped her long locks over her shoulder as if to say her job there was done.

"Well, don't get too excited. At their age, the unease will probably only last about ten minutes," Troy reasoned.

Joy eyed him and then laughed. Once they were in his SUV, she asked again, "Where are we headed?"

"Patience," he said and then didn't say another word until they pulled into the parking lot of the film set.

Joy frowned. "What are we doing here?"

"You'll see." He jumped out of the SUV and actually managed to open her door before she could even undo the seatbelt. He helped her with that too, and once she was on both feet, he took her by the hand and led her to the warehouse that they'd been using as their soundstage for indoor scenes.

"I'm not sure we're supposed to be here," Joy said, glancing around the lot to see if security was watching.

"Joy, it's fine, gorgeous. I got permission." He tapped in a code on the door, and a moment later, he led her inside and she let out a gasp. The entire inside had been transformed into a winter wonderland, complete with an ice-skating rink.

"It's beautiful," she said, turning to him with damp eyes. No one had ever done something like that for her before. "How did you do this?"

"I had a little help from production." He guided her over to a table near the skating rink. Place settings were already laid out with covers over the plates. "Are you hungry?"

"Yes. I had no idea what we were doing, but I assumed dinner at some point."

"You assumed correctly." He removed the covers, and she grinned at him.

"Salmon risotto. The first meal you cooked for me," she said.

"I still remember the look on your face. It does things to me," he said.

Joy leaned over the table and gave him a long, slow, searching kiss, and whispered, "You do things to me." She sat back in her chair and shook her head in wonder. "You miss nothing. The salmon, the ice rink. I told you once that it had been my dream to be a skater when I was a kid and that it still made me happy when I was on the ice." Her gaze shifted to the piles of fake snow and a wooden sled. "That's from when I told you about all the times my mom went sledding with me instead of sending me to school just because she wanted to." Joy scanned the details of the room from the twinkling fairy lights that matched the ones on her own tree perfectly to the funny Santa garden gnome. Each and every detail was a memory of hers from her childhood, and he'd recreated it.

She reached out and clasped his hand. "This is so wonderful, and I love it, but I don't understand. Why did you do all of this? It's not even Christmas."

He gave her a soft, shy smile, and she had to fight the urge to kiss him stupid. It was a problem lately. Anytime he smiled, she wanted him. She was starting to think he'd become an addiction, except neither of them seemed to mind. "When you talk about your childhood, it always comes with a wistfulness, almost an air of longing. Like if you could go back, you would."

Joy pursed her lips and thought about it for a moment. "Maybe. I do miss it. There was such a joy and innocence about winter back in those days. And I do miss the snow."

"Okay, yeah. Well, when I got to thinking about where this

relationship between us is going, I kept coming back to this." He waved a hand at his handiwork.

"That you want to go back to my childhood?" she asked, raising one skeptical eyebrow.

He chuckled. "No. Not at all. I love the adult Joy exactly as she is."

"Love?" she echoed, her entire body tingling. "Did you just say love?" It wasn't something they'd said before. Joy had known her feelings for Troy were strong, but she hadn't been ready to put that out there. Now, though...

"Yes, love. I love you, Joy. I've known it for a while. And I think you love me, too."

"I do," she breathed, placing a hand over her heart. "I love you."

His smile widened. "That's good. Very good." He scanned the room again, and when he met her gaze, he said, "I did all of this to show you that with me, nothing is off the table. If you want the whimsy of your childhood back for the night, I'll do what I can to make it happen. If you want travel, I'll get the tickets to anywhere you want to go, whether that's camping in the Sierras or flying to Italy.

"If your deepest desire is to stay right here in Premonition Pointe for the rest of your days, I'm good with that too. But I might request that you move in with me. Or, if you don't like my house, we'll find another one with a spectacular view, because if there is one thing I know about you, Joy Lansing, it's that you're always in a better mood when you wake up to the sound of the ocean."

There were tears in her eyes, and Joy didn't even bother to try to blink them back. Was this guy the one she loved for real? He was promising her a dream life, *her* dream life, on a silver platter and volunteering to share it with her as a true partner, one who understood her and cared about what she needed. It wasn't something she'd ever had with Paul, and she just prayed that she gave at least half as much back to Troy as he gave to her.

"Your house is perfect," she said through her tears.

"Yeah?" He slipped his hand in hers. "So you'll move in?"

She nodded.

"What about Kyle?"

"Are you inviting him, too?" she asked.

"If it's a dealbreaker, then yes. But we'll need to do some soundproofing."

She laughed and shook her head. "It's not a deal-breaker, and I'm one hundred percent certain he wouldn't want to anyway. He likes when I stay over at your place. He's fine at home. Plus, he'll be moving back to his own apartment soon, and he has Jackson to take care of him."

"That he does." He stood and offered her his hand. "Care to dance?"

She glanced around. "With no music?"

"Alexa, play "The Way You Look Tonight" by Frank Sinatra."

The music came to life, and Joy let Troy lead her around the winter wonderland he'd created just for her. Love and hope and possibility filled her up, made her whole, and she knew deep down that he was the one. Troy was the love of her life, and no matter what happened in their careers or family life, they'd find a way to do it all together and most importantly, do it all while having fun. Her days of walking blindly through her life, waiting for it to get better, were over. She'd found her forever, and she wasn't letting go.

CHAPTER TWENTY-FIVE

$\mathcal{G}$igi Martin held a champagne flute in her hand and watched as her coven, her family as they called themselves, stood in a circle in the lounge of Premonition Pointe's swankiest restaurant. They were laughing and talking and congratulating Grace Valentine on the sale of the gated mansion known as the Emsworth estate that was located ten miles south of town.

Grace, Hope, and Joy really were like the sisters she'd never had. When she'd moved to Premonition Pointe less than a year ago, the three witches whom she loved so much, had opened their hearts to her, pulled her into their fold, and had done so with no questions asked. And for that, she was grateful.

Her past wasn't something she was fond of thinking or talking about. That's what happened when you were married to a narcissistic asshat who didn't think anything of manhandling his wife.

Gigi shuddered at the memories of her ex and then slammed the door on them.

"Gigi!" Hope called. "Get over here, we need you."

"Coming." She made her way over to her friends, Hope and Lucas, Joy and Troy, and Grace and Owen. They were all so beautiful, so happy. Sometimes it was overwhelming, and she started to think of herself as the seventh wheel. It wasn't as if they ever left her out. They didn't. It was just that occasional loneliness that crept up on her when she wasn't paying attention. *Not tonight*, she told herself. *Not tonight.*

"Now that we're all here," Hope said, holding up her flute, "raise your glass to toast the brilliant real estate agent who closed the deal of the century."

"To the brilliant real estate agent," they all said in unison and then downed their champagne. It wasn't long before the glasses were filled again and most of the party ended up sounding tipsy.

"Gigi," Hope said, leaning into her. "I've been meaning to ask you something for a while now."

"Oh, yeah? What's that?" Gigi put her flute down and bent her head closer to Hope so she could hear her.

"How is it that you know that gorgeous lawyer, Sebastian Knight?" She slurred a little when she said Sebastian's name.

Heat flooded Gigi's insides when she pictured the tall man who was Carly Preston's lawyer. It was weird to think of him as someone else's anything when they'd been so close as teenagers. They'd been as close as two people could be without being lovers. Or they were right up until Gigi had been forced to leave town and everyone she loved behind her.

She sighed. That had been a long time ago.

"Gigi?" Hope frowned at her. "Is something wrong?"

"No. Not at all," she said quickly. "I'm just a little tired. You know, long week." Though, really, what did Gigi have to do that made her so tired anyway? She didn't have a job. She didn't need one. Instead, she made potions and lotions and herbs and sold them online just for something to do. Though she did find herself in her earth studio out back quite a bit lately. It really was the only place that seemed to settle her.

"You know what you should do?" Hope asked.

"What's that?" She smiled at her friend, knowing that Hope wasn't feeling much pain in that moment.

"You should let us set you up on a blind date." She grinned triumphantly as if she'd just won something.

"And why would I do that when I can just stay home and cuddle my cat?" Gigi asked. "She's a lot less work and won't think I'm going to get horizontal just because there was dinner involved."

"Um…" Hope's gaze shifted to someone behind Gigi. She glanced at the time on her phone and then grimaced. "Oops. I was a little late on the delivery, Gigi. We already did it. We set you up on a blind date. Surprise."

"What?" Gigi whipped around and then froze when she spotted none other than her old best friend, Sebastian Knight. His dark eyes were full of amusement, and that smile… It was the same one she'd grown up with, only his lips were fuller and a lot more kissable.

Kissable? Where had that come from? Sebastian Knight was not kissable. The man was from her past, and that's where he was supposed to stay.

"Good evening, Gigi," he said, finally getting her chosen name right. The last time they'd run into each other, he'd called her Clarity. The name her mother had given her. The name she'd always hated. But why then, when Sebastian said it, did it sound kind of nice? She shook her head, trying to dislodge the confusing thoughts in her brain.

"It's not a good evening?" he asked.

She stared at him in confusion until his question sank in.

"Yes, it is. Sorry, I was just taken by surprise. It's a very good evening. A great one in fact. We're celebrating Grace's success at work."

"Yes, I heard about that." He glanced at Grace. "Congratulations. I bet you're the envy of the office."

"Even better than that," she said with a laugh. "The other buyer was represented by my ex. So not only did I get the sale, but I get the pleasure of knowing I stole it out from underneath him."

"Serves him right," Hope said. "Cheating bastard."

Grace patted Hope's thigh. "You know it's a true friendship when your girlfriends are even holding grudges."

Everyone laughed and the party resumed, leaving Gigi to deal with her blind date.

"Well, if I promise not to try to get you horizontal, do you think we might give it a try?" Sebastian asked, that glint of humor still shining down at her.

"Give what a try?" she asked like a complete idiot.

"The blind date?"

"Oh, right. Sorry." She waved at the chair across from her at the table, but he took the one on the other side of her where it was quieter.

He ordered a whiskey and soda when the waitress came around and then sat back in the chair, just watching Gigi.

And she didn't like it. His gaze made her uncomfortable, like she was stripped bare and he was seeing all the parts of her she kept hidden from the world.

"You really don't want me here, do you?" he asked.

Gigi closed her eyes and prayed for patience or grace or hell, even courage. "It's not that I don't want you here," she lied. "It's just that I was surprised. I wasn't expecting a date and…" She shrugged. "I'm sure you know how it is when you think you're just going out for a drink and it turns into something completely different."

"Is that what this is?" he asked. "Something different than a drink with a friend? We were friends once, right? We can be again."

It seemed so simple. For most people it probably was. But not for Gigi. Her past was in the past for a reason. And that was damned sure where it was going to stay. She told herself to get to her feet, to get up out of the chair and walk out the door. It's what she was supposed to do. It's what she should've done. But instead, she sat back in her chair, smiled at him, and said, "Yes. We can be friends again."

By the end of the night, Gigi knew she'd had one drink too many. But she hadn't been able to help it. Talking with Sebastian was everything it had been way back when they were teenagers. Easy, fun, intelligent. And he made her laugh, which was extremely rare when one was talking about the opposite sex. For some reason, she had a hard time letting her guard down around most men. But not with him.

She was laughing so hard from a story Sebastian told her about his dating life in college that she barely noticed when her friends stood and were ready to go.

Sebastian looked up at them and smiled. "Is everyone heading out?"

"Yes," Troy said. "This one has to be at the set early." He pointed at Joy and then wrapped his arms around her from behind and nuzzled her neck.

Gigi felt the sigh leave her before she could stop it.

Sebastian eyed her for a moment, and she knew he'd heard it. *Dammit.*

Hope leaned down and whispered, "Looks like my gamble

paid off. You two sure have been having fun. Does this mean you won't hate me in the morning?"

"No. Still going to hate you," Gigi said, but she couldn't help the smile that claimed her lips.

"Uh-huh. I can see that." She stood up again. "Do you need a ride, or is Sebastian going to give you a lift?"

"I can take her home," Sebastian said immediately.

Gigi wanted to protest, because even though she hadn't gotten up and left like she should have, she knew without a doubt that if he took her home she was going to do or say something stupid. Like, *Come on in, Sebastian. Rip my clothes off and have your way with me.*

Nope.

Couldn't happen.

Never going to happen.

She was a liar, liar, pants-on-fire liar, because the moment he pulled into the driveway of her house, she said, "Walk me to my door?"

Being that he was a gentleman, he climbed out of his BMW SUV and came around to open her door. Then he walked her to the vine-covered entryway of her house. "This place is fantastic, Gigi. It reminds me of home."

"Me, too," she said wistfully. "Do you remember the wisteria vines on the treehouse? They were so gorgeous."

"I do. I remember you being livid when your dad chopped them back, too."

She shook her head. "I don't want to think about that." Instead, she nodded to his car. "That doesn't look like a rental."

He shook his head. "Nope. It's not."

"Does that mean you drove up here from LA? Kind of a long drive," she said, suddenly wondering why he was back in

Premonition Pointe at all. She'd assumed he was there to do work for Carly, but now she wasn't sure.

"It would be, if I wasn't staying here through the summer." He glanced around as if taking everything in. "I decided I needed some time away from the city, and Premonition Pointe seemed like a good place for now."

"So you're here for a while," she said, placing one hand on his chest and stepping into him.

"Yeah. Just for a while."

Her heart skipped a beat, and without allowing herself to overthink it, she said, "I'm having second thoughts about getting horizontal with my blind date."

The amusement that she expected to see in his gaze had vanished and been replaced with pure heat. His head came down and his lips covered hers, his tongue tasting, exploring, owning hers.

Gigi melted into him, her arms going around him, and for the first time in years she felt safe in a man's arms. But then he pushed his hand into her hair and tugged. It wasn't painful, nor did she feel threatened by it. But it was enough to send her hurtling back into reality, and she jumped back, putting distance between them.

This could not happen. Not with Sebastian.

"Is something wrong?" he asked, his expressive gaze full of concern.

She shook her head. "No. Sorry. This just isn't…" After sucking in air and blowing it out, she tried again. "This is a mistake. We're old friends. I think it's better if we just call it a night."

He took a step back and shoved his hands in his pockets. "Of course. It's only the first date anyway. I'd never expect to get horizontal until, say, at least the third date."

She blinked at him. Then she laughed. He was such an easy going guy that she imagined if she'd gotten him totally naked and they were seconds from consummating the act and she'd reversed course suddenly, that he'd just nod, make a joke, stuff his junk back into his briefs, and then stroll away whistling as if nothing had ever happened. She laughed again at the imagery.

"What's so funny, Clarity?" he asked softly.

The use of her old name sobered her instantly, and all the reasons she had for needing to keep this man at arm's length came flooding back. "Nothing. Sorry. I should go in. Goodnight, Sebastian. It was good to catch up."

"It was. Maybe we could do this again sometime. Maybe get a meal instead of just a drink?"

She shook her head sadly. "I'm sorry. I don't think I'm interested."

His expression went blank. Then he nodded and said, "I understand. Goodnight, Clar—I mean, Gigi."

She was completely still as she watched Sebastian, the only man she thought she'd ever truly loved, walk out of her life. And it was all her fault.

DEANNA'S BOOK LIST

Witches of Keating Hollow:
Soul of the Witch
Heart of the Witch
Spirit of the Witch
Dreams of the Witch
Courage of the Witch
Love of the Witch
Power of the Witch
Essence of the Witch
Muse of the Witch
Vision of the Witch

Witches of Christmas Grove:
A Witch For Mr. Holiday
A Witch For Mr. Christmas

Premonition Pointe Novels:
Witching For Grace

Witching For Hope
Witching For Joy
Witching For Clarity

Jade Calhoun Novels:
Haunted on Bourbon Street
Witches of Bourbon Street
Demons of Bourbon Street
Angels of Bourbon Street
Shadows of Bourbon Street
Incubus of Bourbon Street
Bewitched on Bourbon Street
Hexed on Bourbon Street
Dragons of Bourbon Street

Pyper Rayne Novels:
Spirits, Stilettos, and a Silver Bustier
Spirits, Rock Stars, and a Midnight Chocolate Bar
Spirits, Beignets, and a Bayou Biker Gang
Spirits, Diamonds, and a Drive-thru Daiquiri Stand
Spirits, Spells, and Wedding Bells

Ida May Chronicles:
Witched To Death
Witch, Please
Stop Your Witchin'

Crescent City Fae Novels:
Influential Magic
Irresistible Magic
Intoxicating Magic

Last Witch Standing:
Bewitched by Moonlight
Soulless at Sunset
Bloodlust By Midnight
Bitten At Daybreak

Witch Island Brides:
The Wolf's New Year Bride
The Vampire's Last Dance
The Warlock's Enchanted Kiss
The Shifter's First Bite

Destiny Novels:
Defining Destiny
Accepting Fate

Wolves of the Rising Sun:
Jace
Aiden
Luc
Craved
Silas
Darien
Wren

Black Bear Outlaws:
Cyrus
Chase
Cole

Bayou Springs Alien Mail Order Brides:

Zeke

Gunn

Echo

ABOUT THE AUTHOR

New York Times and USA Today bestselling author, Deanna Chase, is a native Californian, transplanted to the slower paced lifestyle of southeastern Louisiana. When she isn't writing, she is often goofing off with her husband in New Orleans or playing with her two shih tzu dogs. For more information and updates on newest releases visit her website at deannachase.com.

Made in the USA
Middletown, DE
07 October 2020